... you ... asked Lucy, taking a cup of tea. I could see that she could barely wait to answer her own question.

'Who? Do tell!' I replied.

'Why, the Honourable Johnny Hughes, no less!' giggled Lucy.

'Ah, the *Adorable* Johnny Hughes!' I laughed, mentioning a nickname often used for him. 'We might meet him at last! He is, by all accounts, this season's "must-have" accessory – but what makes him so special, do you know?' I enquired.

'Well, let's see now . . . They say he's the handsomest man in England! And one of the wealthiest. My sister Catherine saw him at a masked ball at Carlton House last autumn – without the mask, I should add – and she said he was simply dreamy,' Lucy told me eagerly. 'Plus, my maid, Daisy, who you know came to us from the Earl of Oxford's country estate, says that she has seen Mr Hughes, and that he is a rare mixture of strong and gentle, with a handsome face and a tall broad frame. And, what is more, simply *everyone* says he has a warm, good heart! Oh, Sophie, it *must* be true!' L.M.R

The Secrets of Sophia Musgrove

Dancing and Deception

JANEY LOUISE JONES

CORGI BOOKS

DANCING AND DECEPTION
A CORGI BOOK 978 0 552 55822 8

Published in Great Britain by Corgi Books,
an imprint of Random House Children's Books
A Random House Group Company

This edition published 2009

Set in 13.5/17pt Adobe Garamond Pro by
Falcon Oast Graphic Art Ltd.

Corgi Books are published by Random House Children's Books,
61–63 Uxbridge Road, London W5 5SA

www.kidsatrandomhouse.co.uk
www.rbooks.co.uk

Addresses for companies within The Random House Group Limited can be found at:
www.randomhouse.co.uk/offices.htm

THE RANDOM HOUSE GROUP Limited Reg. No. 954009

A CIP catalogue record for this book is available from the British Library.

Printed in the UK by CPI Bookmarque, Croydon, CR0 4TD

For Amber Caravéo,
with grateful thanks for all her help

ENGLAND, 1803

Chapter One

I had just returned from a most successful shopping trip in Mayfair with Mrs Willow, who is my mother's cousin and my governess-turned-chaperone, when our butler appeared and announced the arrival of two guests. It was chilly out and I was warming my hands by the roaring log fire in the receiving room of Musgrove House.

'Hurrah! Visitors! Who are they, Hawkes?' I asked.

'It is Lady Lucy Pennington, accompanied by Lady Lennox,' he replied, looking nearly as pleased as I was. My best friend, Lucy, has this cheering effect on everyone she meets – even Dinky, my sweet little King Charles spaniel.

'Lucy! Yippee! Well, show her in at once please,' I said as Mrs Willow quickly put on her indoor lace cap – ever mindful of the fine social standing of Lucy's aunt, Lady Lennox. 'And send Annie in with tea, please,' I added as Hawkes withdrew. I had not seen my best friend for more than a month as she had been in the Lake District at one of her family's country homes. I couldn't wait to hear all her news.

Lucy burst through the door, beaming from ear to ear and carrying a vast array of bags from various stores around Piccadilly. She looked as pretty as usual, wearing a deep-rose-pink coat fastened over a biscuit-coloured day dress of the new Greek cut which, being less fitted than the traditional style, hung elegantly on her tall slim figure. Lucy is quite beautiful, and her French-style bonnet framed her peachy complexion and wide blue eyes perfectly. Lucy always has the nicest clothes in London.

Lady Lennox trotted behind with more bags, looking rather dull in comparison to her charge, in a grey wool outer coat.

'Greetings!' cried Lucy as she handed her bonnet and coat to Hawkes and came to hug me warmly. 'Look what I've got, Sophia!' she said, reaching into her reticule and pulling out an invitation to Queen Charlotte's annual ball. 'Do you have one yet?'

'How exciting! The ball is next Saturday, isn't it? My invitation hasn't arrived yet, but perhaps the Queen's office simply gave it to my mother. I'll check. In the meantime' – I turned to Mrs Willow –

'perhaps you would like to entertain Lady Lennox in the drawing room, Mrs Willow?' I suggested, hopeful of some privacy. But Mrs Willow frowned. She loves to hear all the latest news – especially from Lucy, who knows *everybody* in London society and relates all the stories about them with such humour.

'No need to heat another room just now, Sophia, dear. We will stay in the warmth and catch up on all the news,' she replied. 'But don't worry, we won't eavesdrop. Lady Lennox and I have our own interesting lives to discuss!'

'I don't believe it,' muttered Lucy under her breath with a giggle. Our chaperones are employed to accompany us in public at all times and keep us out of trouble, since our parents cannot always be with us. My mother is often away at Kew, where she is chief lady-in-waiting to Queen Charlotte, which means that she plans the Queen's diary and co-ordinates her clothes, amongst many other duties. Lucy's mother is always busy with her huge family. Lady Pennington simply loves having babies, and as they grow bigger, she somehow forgets about them, or so it seems. But our chaperones, Mrs Willow and Lady Lennox, make sure we are never alone for long – unfortunately!

'*We* were never taken on shopping trips to fancy

stores, were we, Clarissa?' said Mrs Willow with a smile, moving to the other end of our vast receiving room and settling herself down on one of the sofas with Lady Lennox.

'No indeed, Annabel,' replied Lady Lennox, and soon they were chatting happily about the many new luxuries we enjoy today, and Lucy and I were able to talk freely by the fire at last.

'Can you guess who is going to be at the ball?' asked Lucy, taking a cup of tea provided by Annie, our sweet new general maid. I could see that she could barely wait to answer her own question.

'Who? Do tell!' I replied.

'Why, the Honourable Johnny Hughes, no less!' giggled Lucy.

'Ah, the *Adorable* Johnny Hughes!' I laughed, mentioning a nickname often used for him. 'We might meet him at last! He is, by all accounts, this season's "must-have" accessory – but what makes him so special, do you know?' I enquired.

'Well, let's see now . . . They say he's the hand-somest man in England! And one of the wealthiest. *And,* what's more, he's a real man, not a dandy like the insufferable Prince of Wales!'

'Well, that has to be a good thing,' I said. 'The Prince is a bit too much in love with himself for my liking.' I often bump into the Prince in the corridors of the White House when I am visiting Mama at Kew. He always seems incredibly vain to me, and the gossip columns in the newspapers confirm my suspicions. 'But, Lucy,' I continued, 'since we've never seen this Mr Hughes ourselves, how can we be sure that all this wonderful talk about him is true?'

'Well, my sister Catherine saw him at a masked ball at Carlton House last autumn – without the mask, I should add – and she said he was simply dreamy,' Lucy told me eagerly. 'Plus, my maid, Daisy, who you know came to us from the Earl of Oxford's country estate, says that she has seen Mr Hughes many times at weekend parties there, and that he is a rare mixture of strong and gentle, with a handsome face and a tall broad frame. And, what is more, simply *everyone* says he has a warm, good heart! Oh, Sophie, it *must* be true!'

'Hmm, I should like to see him with my own eyes,' I said cautiously, although I was very intrigued, to tell the truth. 'He is very elusive – what with his military career taking him abroad all the time. If all this *is* true, then he sounds like a proper hero, I agree! Oh, Lucy, just imagine, if he has been decorated in battle as well, then he would be the *perfect* gentleman!'

'You are right!' Lucy agreed. 'But what am I thinking of?' she cried, suddenly bending to rummage through her bags. 'I've been here a full ten minutes and haven't yet shown you my purchases!'

I leaned forward eagerly; we both so love to shop at the magnificent new stores in Pall Mall and Piccadilly. Even though most of our dresses are made by our mothers' dressmakers, there are still shoes, reticules, perfumes and jewellery to find.

'What do you think of these little beauties?' exclaimed Lucy, pulling a pair of exquisite satin shoes from one of her bags. 'One size too small, but well worth the Ugly Sister squeeze!'

'They are quite heavenly,' I breathed, admiring the shapely high heels and lace trim. 'They look incredibly French!'

'Exactly,' said Lucy. 'I know we are supposed to hate the French because of the blessed war and all their revolutionary ways, but I, for one, say: *Vive la France!* They are quite the most stylish people! Who cares about their politics? If Queen Marie-Antoinette hadn't been so thoughtless, they wouldn't have chopped off her head, would they?'

We giggled. This was treasonous talk – almost. But we often drooled over Parisian fashion magazines and begged our dressmakers to copy the styles, which they invariably declared to be 'common' and 'vulgar' and 'impractical'.

'Oh, that reminds me,' I said. 'I went shopping myself this morning – and picked a French hat for my sister's wedding! Would you like to see it?'

'Ooh, yes please!' cried Lucy. 'Do go and get it, Sophie!'

The hat was still in its glorious satin box in the hallway and I ran to put it on. I re-entered the receiving room in fashion-plate mode, posing daintily and tilting my head from side to side.

'Sophia, I love it. It frames your face perfectly. Your shiny brown curls look gorgeous under it and I am so jealous of your long dark lashes. Of course, Estella will steal the show – that is only proper – but you will be almost as spectacular in that delicious French confection!' Lucy declared.

'Isn't it perfect? But I have to be careful,' I told her. 'If my father hears me admiring anything French he makes me wash out my mouth with soap and water. He is fiercely loyal to the Prime Minister, Mr Addington, who you know is always raising taxes to fight the French.' I sighed. 'The only good aspect of war, as far as I can see, is the dashing soldiers' uniforms,' I concluded.

Lucy nodded in whole-hearted agreement and

reached for another shopping bag. This was a work of art in itself, made of chintz cloth, hand-embroidered with silk stitching in violet, lilac and old-rose pink. Inside was a huge selection of lotions and perfumes set in a pink silk-lined box.

'These are the very latest creams we've been waiting for, Sophie,' Lucy explained.

'Oh, I've been wanting them for ages. Allington's didn't have any. Where did you manage to find them?' I asked.

'In The Rosewater Company,' Lucy replied. 'This is Milk of Rose. And see, this one is Bloom of Ninon. And at the end of the routine you must apply the Morning Dew as a tonic,' she explained.

I was impressed, for I had read all about all these potions in the *Lady's Magazine*. 'Can I try some?' I asked.

Lucy nodded and carefully undid the caps. 'This will make your skin really soft – and your lips too,' she said. 'You are lucky as you have rosebud lips to start with.'

'Me? Do I? I wish I had a large, full smile like yours,' I said. The creams smelled wonderfully fragrant and we enjoyed dabbling with them as we chatted.

'I presume your mother is at Court just now, Sophie?' Lucy asked.

'Yes, unfortunately,' I replied. 'I miss her so much. We are hoping she will be back with us next month, but in the meantime we have to make do with visiting her at the White House, which is a trial, I can assure you.' I lowered my voice as I continued. 'The King is totally cuckoo just now, Lucy. He scares me a little when he is over from Kew Palace. He thinks I'm Princess Amelia, his youngest daughter, and often tries to kiss me!'

'Ugh!' exclaimed Lucy. 'That is the most repulsive thing I've ever heard! He's *ancient*.'

'Exactly!' I agreed, shuddering dramatically. 'And he thinks that one of the noble ladies at Court, Lady Pemberton, is his wife, and he doesn't recognize the poor Queen at all – though she has borne him fifteen children!'

'Oh, it sounds like a madhouse. Why doesn't your mother just stop being a lady-in-waiting?' wondered Lucy.

'Because it is an "honour"!' I sighed. 'I wish heartily that my father would *not* allow her to put herself out so much for the Queen, but as a politician he must maintain his social position and so Mama's role at Court suits him well. And,' I conceded, 'I really think she pities the Queen. It is a sad state of affairs for the Royal Family. Do you to know a secret?' I asked, lowering my voice.

'Naturally,' said Lucy, who can never resist a tasty morsel of gossip.

'Well, the King will not let the older Princesses be wooed by foreign Princes in case they must move overseas, so they sometimes have romances with their servants!'

Lucy's eyes widened in surprise, for this was really shocking. Young ladies like ourselves have to romance suitable gentlemen from our own circle, and the Royals are expected to have even higher standards.

Just then, Hawkes came into the receiving room with a letter.

'Aha! This will no doubt be your invitation to the ball, Sophia,' said Lucy gleefully. 'And not before time, with only a few days to go!'

Hawkes cleared his throat. 'It's a message from the Royal Court, Miss Sophia. An urgent message. You must read it at once!' he said.

I did not think that a belated ball invitation could be classed as an 'urgent message' so I felt a little worried as I took the letter.

Mrs Willow and Lady Lennox joined us hastily from the other end of the room and I broke open the royal seal on the back of the envelope and read the note aloud:

'The White House
Kew

The fourth day of April, 1803
For the urgent attention of Miss Sophia
Musgrove

Dear Miss Musgrove,
As your older sister is in the country, we have been
asked by your mother to contact you directly. We
are sorry to inform you that your mother, Lady
Musgrove, has been taken seriously ill at the
White House. She has asked for you to attend her.
We would be pleased if you could come to her
bedside with the greatest haste. We have notified
your father also.

Yours,
Charles Lacomb, Esquire
Surgeon to the Royal Court'

Lucy gasped and clutched her throat.
'We must go to her at once!' I said shakily.
Mrs Willow came over to embrace me. 'All will be
well, Sophie, when we remove her from that royal
madhouse. Fear not, dear child. Hawkes, please have
Ted bring the carriage round to the front door at

once, and ask Lily to prepare Miss Musgrove's outdoor things.'

'At once, ma'am,' said Hawkes, looking somewhat dazed by the unexpected turn of events.

'Sophia,' continued Mrs Willow, 'prepare yourself and we will meet at the front door in five minutes. Lady Lennox, Lady Lucy, I regret that we must bid you farewell,' she said calmly, and I felt a rush of affection for her orderly, dependable nature.

Lucy embraced me, as did her aunt, and they left as swiftly as they had arrived – with expressions of concern for my mother, of course. I went straight to my room, where my maid, Lily, was currently filling my best embroidered reticule with a handkerchief, comb and coins. I saw that she had already brushed down my green wool coat.

'Oh, Miss Sophia, is Her Ladyship very bad?' Lily asked, full of concern. Her own mother had died just a year ago.

'Lily, I can't say,' I told her. 'I have to see her, that's all I know – especially as I fear Papa will be too caught up in political debate at Westminster to attend her straight away.'

'May I come with you?' asked Lily shyly.

'Yes, Lily, please do,' I said, grateful for the moral

support. 'Go and tell the housekeeper of your departure and fetch your warm coat.'

'Right you are, miss,' said Lily, clearly glad to be of help. 'I'll meet you in the carriage.'

How will we tell Estella? I worried to myself as I tidied my hair, which Lily had earlier pinned in a loose topknot. I automatically took off my fashionable hairband and put on my shako-style high hat trimmed with ostrich feathers. *It will take a day to get a message to her at the Daisy Park* – this is our country residence near Cheltenham, where Estella was preparing for her forthcoming marriage. My little brother, Harry, was at school. I was anxious about my siblings being kept in the dark, but even more concerned about Mama. I decided to concentrate on her well-being for now, which I knew was what my sister and brother would want. There would be time enough to inform them of her condition when we knew more about it.

I rushed downstairs and out to the carriage, which stood waiting on the cobbled London street. Mrs Willow and Lily were nowhere to be seen so I paced up and down impatiently in front of the elegant stone townhouses under the sympathetic gaze of Ted, our kind young coachman.

The others soon appeared and at last we set off. I

felt quite dizzy with fear. I knew that Mama must be very ill for the Queen's surgeon to send for us. I simply could not bear the thought of losing her.

As our carriage rattled and swayed at top speed through the streets of London, I prayed that all would be well – and feared that it would not!

Chapter Two

*I*t seemed to take an eternity to reach Kew, but when we did I was struck all over again by how plain the White House is. It's so simple in style, like a child's drawing of a house. There was a small welcoming party standing on the steps, which alarmed us all even more. I jumped out of the carriage and ran towards the entrance in a most unladylike fashion. The housekeeper, Mrs Feathers, greeted us. 'Come in, come in, Miss Sophia! She is asking for you every minute, they tell me!' she explained.

Inside, members of the Royal Household were in a state of controlled panic. I knew from the expressions on their faces, and the fact that the doors between the apartments were locked, that the King was in residence, rather than being at Kew Palace as usual, and that he was having one of his mad episodes. I had seen all the signs during previous visits, and Mama had told me about his antics on many occasions.

The royal children were employed in playing games and drawing, even though most are past childhood. Some wore heavy boots, ready for their daily walks across the park. They all have a tendency to gain weight, which is countered with various exercise regimes. Two of the older Princesses were posing for a portrait in the galleried hallway as we passed by, en route to my mother's chambers. I recognized the artist as Thomas Lawrence – my family had sat for him just last year.

As we entered the private wing where the Queen and her ladies-in-waiting sleep, we bumped into the Prince of Wales. We all curtsied, of course, and he asked Mrs Feathers about a dinner party he was hosting that evening.

I silently fizzed with frustration. Mama lay suffering and we had to stand here conversing with an obese buffoon caked in make-up about the merits of duck pie and quince crumble!

We soon excused ourselves and made haste through a maze of corridors to my mother's chamber. As we stood outside the door, I could hear the Queen's loud German accent. I prepared myself for our meeting by carefully thinking kind and sweet thoughts about her. I knew that she would interpret this turn of events as her own personal misfortune, and that any sign of frustration on my part would only make things worse. What would she do without my wonderful mother – sensible, mild-mannered Maria Musgrove?

As Mrs Feathers opened the door to Mama's sleeping chamber, I was dismayed by the sight before me. She lay limply against a pile of white pillows, with a grey pallor and a pasty look to her small, heart-shaped face. She was forty-two years of age, but looked more like sixty. At one side of her bed stood the Queen, looking agitated, and at the other was Mr Lacomb, the royal surgeon. He appeared to be taking blood from a vein in my poor mother's forearm. My mother's devoted maid, Lottie, also looked on in distress.

'Mama, dearest!' I cried, almost forgetting to curtsy to the Queen as I hastened to her bedside. I corrected myself hurriedly, thus tripping and nearly falling headlong onto the bed myself.

Mrs Willow and Lily also drew close to my mother, offering words of sympathy and comfort. I could see that she knew we were there as she opened her eyes and tried to smile. She mouthed the words: 'Sophie, darling.'

'How long has she been like this, Mr Lacomb?' I asked the surgeon, who was now binding her arm tightly with bandages.

'Several days, but she is getting weaker, Miss Musgrove. We were convinced that she would improve – and she kept going for a while as she was much needed during the recent visit of the Queen's brother and his large family from Germany. As you know, the Queen relies on your mother to organize social events and keep the peace between the royal children and their guests when there are visitors at Court. They left last night, and only then did we realize how weak Lady Maria had become,' he explained.

Mrs Willow tutted loudly and pursed her lips into an O-shape. I felt furious with the Queen for exploiting Mama's good nature like this, but I bit my tongue, knowing that anger would not make her well again.

'Oh, mercy me!' cried the Queen. 'I will never cope without my Maria. You must make her well, Lacomb. For all our sakes!'

'I will do all I can, Your Majesty, but she requires complete rest and quiet,' he replied firmly.

At this point the King burst in through the door, turning like a spinning top and babbling as though he were a lunatic. He was wearing a long white cotton nightshirt and his bald head was wigless, making him look very old indeed. As usual, an entourage of four restrainers accompanied him in case he should become violent or obscene.

'My people are trying to kill me, Charlotte! They shot at me, you know, in broad daylight. With a gun! A large gun! Their own king! They hate Addington and the wars, and now I am to blame, apparently,' he raved. 'Of course, it goes back to me losing the Americas, what, what!'

I looked curiously at Mr Lacomb. 'It's all quite true,' he confirmed. 'His Majesty was out in his coach yesterday when a shot missed him by a fraction of an inch. The people of England are greatly angered by the loss of the Americas and the taxes being levied for the war.'

That's the odd thing about the King. At times he will speak the truth, but then, within seconds, he will be spouting utter gibberish.

The Queen smiled benignly, perhaps pleased that he had remembered her name in a little lucid moment, but she said nothing. It was as though the fact that he had been shot at went right over her head.

'Ah, Amelia!' the King said suddenly, looking at me. 'My dearest, sweetest child! What, what!' I looked at the men in his entourage a little nervously, hoping they might intervene, but it seemed they had no power to influence him and merely hovered around him wherever he went.

'We just saw the Prince of Wales in the corridor, Your Majesty,' I said, in an effort to distract him. 'He was looking for you.'

I think we all prayed he would take the bait. 'The Prince! Here, in the White House? I must find that damnable boy and tell him a thing or two! Trying to take the crown from my head. My own flesh and blood! The rogue! The usurper!' And the King spun on his heels and stormed from the room, followed by his team of sheep.

'I must follow him!' said the Queen. 'They fight like cat and dog, my husband and my son.'

It was a relief to be free of the royal couple. The surgeon stayed with us, too loyal to express his own feelings at the departure of the King and Queen, but plainly delighted to be released from their presence, if only for a few moments.

I pulled a chair towards my mother and sat down, talking quietly to her. 'Would you like to come back to Musgrove House, Mama, dear?' I asked her. She nodded, her eyes still shut tight. I looked at Mr Lacomb.

'Perhaps in the morning,' he suggested. 'A journey at the moment would destabilize her further. If you can make sure she has complete rest for several hours, and plenty of boiled, cooled water, then I will check on her before breakfast. I suggest you have your own doctor in attendance at your residence. She needs a great deal of care.'

'But what is wrong with her, sir?' I asked.

'I can't give it a name yet, Miss Musgrove, but the symptoms are becoming clearer: extreme nausea, exhaustion and cramps,' he said.

A mystery illness! I was terrified, for how could we treat a sickness we did not understand? I had an irrational idea that the King's illness might be contagious, but I dismissed that silly notion from my mind as a messenger arrived with a letter from Papa.

As I had suspected, his letter was kind but said that he was unable to leave Westminster. I felt a pang of annoyance on my mother's behalf, but Mrs Willow read the letter aloud to her and she smiled contentedly at her husband's words.

Ted drove Lily back to Musgrove House to fetch night clothes for herself, Mrs Willow and me, and the three of us, plus Lottie, slept in my mother's apartment, taking turns to attend to her and willing her to be strong enough to come back home with us in the morning.

At daybreak I was woken by the strong accent of the Queen. I stood up quickly and curtsied.

'Ah! She's better. Thank God!' she declared on seeing my mother.

I looked at Mama, who seemed to me just as frail and grey as before, and exchanged anxious glances with Mrs Willow, Lottie and Lily.

'I'm sorry, Your Majesty, but she will take longer than this to recover. We must take her home with us to Musgrove House today,' I said softly. Mrs Willow, Lottie and Lily drew closer behind me, offering silent support.

The Queen let out a little shriek. 'All my dear ladies are deserting me!' she cried. 'Lady Catherine is no longer teaching the children. She *says* her son is ill . . .'

I happened to know that young Lord Winchilsea was in fact dying, and his mother was nursing him as best she could, but I knew better than to argue with the Queen, so I kept my head down and was grateful when Mr Lacomb appeared and insisted that Mama must have quiet if she was to recover.

Mercifully the Queen wandered out of the

chamber, muttering, 'Everyone is deserting me. What have I done to deserve it?'

Mr Lacomb examined Mama carefully. 'If we wrap her up well against the cold, then I believe she can be moved today to a place of rest,' he concluded.

What a relief it would be for all of us to leave the stifling Royal Court and return to the sanctuary of our own dear home. I almost wished I could take poor Mr Lacomb with us too and give him a break from the madhouse.

Two footmen carried my mother out to our carriage, and Ted drove us home sedately over the cobbles, mindful of the bumps that might jar her. I felt my heart lift as our house came into sight. Surely once she was safe at home with us to nurse her, Mama would soon recover.

Chapter Three

When we entered Musgrove House, my father was waiting to greet us. He is tall and always stands very straight. This, together with his greying hair and moustache, gives him an imposing look. If I didn't know and love him, I think I'd find him rather frightening. He looked unmoved on the surface, but I was pleased that he had made sure he was there for Mama's return, and when I studied him more closely I could see that he was shaken to see her in such ill-health.

My mother's face lit up when Papa kissed her and helped to carry her to her room.

Once Mama was comfortably settled in her own bedroom, with my father at her side, we all gathered round her bed. Papa stroked her hand gently, then seemed to realize that they were not alone and blushed.

'Well, this is not getting on with the business of government, is it, Maria?' he said, looking at his watch.

Mama simply smiled indulgently. 'Off you go, Hugo. I don't mind. I need to rest,' she told him.

'I trust we have all the right medical people attending to my dear wife?' he said to our housekeeper, Mrs Merry, who nodded.

Papa turned to me and embraced me rather awkwardly. 'Well done, Sophie, dear. It was good of you to go and fetch your mother. You are turning into a very fine young lady,' he said stiffly.

I smiled. This was a huge compliment from my father. I thought I felt him tremble with emotion, but when he let go of me he was as calm as ever.

Dinky settled down for a nap next to Mama, who adores him, and I retired to my room to attend to the pile of mail that was waiting for me. Firstly, there was a letter from Lucy:

5th April, 9 o'clock of the morning

My dear Sophie,
 When it suits you, please do give us news of your dear mother. We are thinking of you all.

I will visit again on Friday, unless it does not suit.

Your loving friend, Lucy, all the Penningtons, and Clarissa Lennox xxx

Another envelope contained the invitation to the Queen's ball. It was very grand.

Her Majesty, Queen Charlotte,
requests the pleasure of the company of
MISS SOPHIA MUSGROVE
At her Annual Ball
In the Ballroom at Grosvenor House,
101 Buckingham Palace Road, London
Saturday, 8th April
7 o'clock
Carriages at midnight
RSVP
The Royal Household
St James's Palace
London

The ball has been held annually since 1780, when the King gave a society ball for the Queen's birthday, and I have mixed feelings about it. On the one hand, I resent the whole idea of the social Season and the way that debutantes such as Lucy and I are set before the eligible young men of the country in the hope that matches will be made. It is rather embarrassing to be involved in such a 'marriage parade'. And yet all the balls and parties are so much fun, and as my thoughts wandered to the elusive Mr Hughes I realized that I desperately wanted to go to the ball and see what he was like for myself. But then I remembered my mother's condition and immediately felt guilty for thinking about the ball at all.

The third piece of mail was from my sister, Estella.

The Daisy Park
Whistling Sparrows
Nr Cheltenham

4th April 1803

My dearest Sophie,

I am having such fun planning the wedding out here in the country, but I do miss you terribly. I'm not sure if I was right to go for a country wedding, but Percy – dear Percy – says it is more convenient for all his family. My future in-laws have arrived from Oxford and are staying with Lord Sandford at Mellorbay Hall, across the park. They are very interested in the wedding arrangements and are helping me enormously. I only wish that Mama were here, with her keen and tasteful eye. Have you been to Court to see her lately?

My idea for the after-wedding party is to create a 'fairy glade' in the garden by the lake, and light it with lanterns for the evening. Dear old Mr Mackle is helping with the garden. We are quite obsessive about plants and shrubs just now! Don't I sound dull? Thank goodness I have Miss Bowes to keep me company and help with the plans. She is a dear companion.

Have you chosen your hat yet? I will be making a little posy of garden flowers for you to carry, and as soon as you arrive, we will commence with the dress fittings in the village. As you know, my dress is on order from Paris. I'm so pleased I chose the one you liked best. As for reticules, what do you think? Please let me know.

I am so lucky to have Percy; even though he gets a little cross at times, he is every girl's dream. Have you any suitors? Are you going to the Queen's ball? That's where I met my Percy!
Do write soon – and more often!

Your loving sister,
Estella xxx

I sighed. I didn't want to alarm Estella about Mama. She would certainly come to London immediately. And as for our brother, Harry, he was only eight and had just settled at pre-naval school, after a period of homesickness, so I didn't want to trouble him either. But as I read to my mother that afternoon – from *The Mysteries of Udolpho* by the thrilling novelist, Mrs Radcliffe – I had a brilliant idea.

Wouldn't Mama heal better in the country air? Perhaps we should repair to the Daisy Park, where the air was purer and the stresses of Court life seemed a million miles away – and where wedding fever was in the air. This plan would also save Estella from coming up to London. I decided to suggest this to Papa at supper.

I waited until we were eating our apple pie and chantilly-cream puddings to bring up the subject. He was all in favour of the idea – anything so that he could get on with his tedious politics uninterrupted, I thought! So it was decided that Ted and a groom, Matthew, would drive Mrs Willow, Lily, Lottie and me to Cheltenham with Mama three days later. Naturally, Dinky would come too.

I had sent a message to Lucy explaining my mother's illness as best I could and confirming that she should visit as she had suggested in her letter. It was a breath of fresh air when she came running into the morning room that Friday shortly after breakfast.

What a lot had happened since our impromptu tea party on Tuesday when Lucy had dropped in with Lady Lennox.

'Lucy! It's wonderful to see you. Please cheer me up!' I said by way of greeting.

'Oh, I see. What am I? The Court jester? Or the village idiot?' complained Lucy with a twinkle in her eye.

'I *did* get my invitation to the ball,' I told her, pointing to the over-mantel where it sat. 'But sadly I will miss it, Lucy, for it is tomorrow, and first thing in the morning I am to travel to our Cotswolds house with Mama. We are to spend time with Estella and we hope the change of air will do Mama some good.'

'How is she, dear lady?' asked Lucy. She truly loves my mother, as everyone does, because Mama is always interested in our thoughts and feelings.

'She is no better, but no worse,' I said. It was truly an unfathomable situation. She was nauseous, weak and tired, but on odd occasions could almost be her old self.

'Of course, your mother's well-being must come first,' Lucy said, 'but what a shame about the ball!

Your dance with the Honourable Johnny has come to nothing!'

'How do you know he would want to dance with me?' I asked.

'Sophia! Look at yourself,' Lucy replied firmly. 'You are the prettiest girl this season!' I think she was trying to cheer me up after my terrible week.

'Nonsense!' I laughed. Lucy is ten times prettier than me. And I think scores of other society girls are lovelier too.

'Well, if you can't come to the ball, then I shall travel down to the Daisy Park and tell you all about it. How's that?' suggested Lucy.

'Oh, that sounds absolutely perfect!' I exclaimed. 'And you'd better have lots of details about Mr Hughes. Real live facts, I mean,' I added.

'Fear not,' said Lucy with a gleam in her eye. 'My mission is to have his name on my dance card by nine o'clock!'

Chapter Four

We set off for the country on the Saturday morning about ten o'clock, with all manner of articles attached to the top of the coach, as we would now be in the country until the wedding in a month's time. I tried to banish all thoughts of missing the ball from my mind. We took leave of my father and he waved us out of the courtyard of Musgrove House.

Mama was propped up comfortably in the corner of our largest carriage, which was not the smartest one, but ideal for a rough cross-country journey in early April. She was lying against pillows and quilts, all wrapped up in layers and looking like a tiny swaddled baby. Lottie fussed over her sweetly.

I had sent a message ahead to Estella, so she would know to expect us. In it, I told her about Mama's illness too. We wanted the house to be ready for her, with a doctor in attendance, and we also wanted Estella to be prepared for her condition.

Mrs Willow was overseeing the mini-removal – she was wonderfully efficient. My mother relied on her too, and felt better when she was around. Lily was quite excited about the trip to the country, for she had never been out of London. I felt my spirits lift as we left the city as well. I was sure Mama would soon feel better once we were at the Daisy Park.

Just outside Oxford, we stopped for refreshments and to change the horses. The coaching inn, called the Black Mare, was a little rough, but Mama needed to rest. They served us with freshly baked bread, a hot stew and local cheese, with apples and pickles. Lottie accompanied my mother to a private room to put her feet up, while Mrs Willow and I ate in the snug, where there was quite a buzz of chatter and a blazing fire by which to warm ourselves.

'Where are you bound?' asked a local man.

'Cheltenham area,' replied our coachman, Ted.

'Well, watch yourselves, for there's a highwayman at large. Plaguing the gateway to the Cotswolds, so he is. And he's cunning. He's felled the occupants of many a fancy coach with his wily ways. So be warned, driver, stop for no one on ill-lit pathways and take no risks!' said the man.

Going out into the yard again, I found Lily and Matthew and told them the news about the highwayman, and then gave them a basket of food from the inn. We all made ready for the next stage of the journey. We said goodbye to our beloved horses, Silverbell and Cloud. Of course, we would see them again soon. Once they were rested, a postillion rider would bring them on to the Daisy Park.

As the evening wore on, Lily, Lottie, Mrs Willow and I all dozed, along with Mama – the effects of the food and wine, no doubt. But I was jerked awake by a sudden cry from Ted.

'There's an injured rider ahead!' he shouted down to us.

We peered out of the window, trying to make out the scene on the narrow country road ahead.

I saw a figure lying in the road, and then we heard a feeble voice begging for help. 'Can you help a poor man with a broken leg?' the stranger cried. 'I've been stuck here for half a day or more and I'm losing blood. My horse has stood faithfully by my side, but he's hungry and weak.'

Lily frowned. I guessed that she was still thinking of the warning from the coaching inn. But my mother was very keen to stop and aid the traveller.

'Poor soul – the least we can do is take him to the nearest doctor!' she said.

By now, Ted had slowed down somewhat. I gazed at the stranger as we drew closer, trying to work out if he was to be trusted. I didn't want to be heartless, but the warnings from the Black Mare were fresh in my mind. The man called out for mercy, but still I could not see his face, which was turned away from us at an odd angle.

From the way he held himself I could not be sure that he *was* in pain. And when I looked at his horse I thought that it did not look like a creature which had spent half a day without food or water. At this point, Dinky, who was sitting on my lap, growled ominously.

'Ted,' I shouted out, my mind made up. 'Remember the warning at the inn! Do not stop. Drive on!'

Mama looked aghast, but as our coach rattled past, I called from the window to the traveller: 'We will send help from the next coaching inn. We already have an invalid on board and have no space!'

'Sophia, how uncharitable!' scolded my mother. 'We could have squeezed up and made space.'

But we all looked back along the road as we

sped away from the scene and my mother gasped.

'Oh, my dear! I'm so sorry. You were right!' she cried, falling back upon her cushions, for the 'injured' man was now standing up in the middle of the road – clearly uninjured – and as he turned towards us, a shaft of moonlight revealed the black mask of a highwayman across his eyes!

We travelled on through the night and into the next morning, with Matthew taking the reins from Ted every so often. Poor Mrs Willow continued to fret about highwaymen.

'Mrs Willow, I don't think anyone will dare take on Miss Sophia and Lily Vallant!' joked Ted when we stopped to change horses at Moreton. 'Not if he knows what's good for him!' He winked at Lily, who blushed and giggled.

As the rising sun bathed the early morning landscape, we clip-clopped into the quaint Cotswold village of Whistling Sparrows, and within minutes were bowling along the drive of the Daisy Park. It was lovely to see the sweet old manor house ahead in the distance, and nicer still to think of seeing darling Estella when we reached it.

Mama pinched her cheeks to give them colour and tidied herself, ready to meet her eldest child. And then we saw Estella running down the driveway to greet us, having heard the horses' hooves in the quiet of the early morning. She looked a picture in her flowing sprig-patterned muslin dress, with her blonde hair flying loose in the breeze. Ted slowed the carriage and Estella dived in on top of us. Mrs Willow rebuked her gently.

'Your mother is in a delicate state, dear child. Be careful!' she said with a warm smile.

Estella covered our mother in kisses and jumped back out of the coach as we drew to a halt outside the house. We all climbed out as the coachmen and some servants began to unload our luggage.

'Mind the wedding hat, you clumsy carthorse!' called Lily to Ted, in a fit of giggles.

'Did she say *wedding hat?*' asked Estella. 'Oooh, do let me see it!'

Mama smiled, watching Estella and me walking arm in arm as she was carefully carried into the house by Ted and Matthew, with Lottie fussing at her side.

Our life in the city seemed so far away as we set about bringing our country bedrooms to life, catching up on bits of local news, and, of course, engaging in wedding chit-chat. We usually stay in the country for two months at a time, although these were rather unusual circumstances, what with the wedding and Mama's illness.

Lily was a dear: she went about her duties quietly, arranging our favourite things exactly how we wanted them. On our arrival Miss Bowes, Estella's companion, took the opportunity to return to the rectory and visit her elderly parents.

I told Estella about our brush with the highwayman. 'If he had triumphed over us, we would have lost all Mama's jewels for the wedding,' I commented.

'Never mind the jewels, what if you'd been injured?' gasped Estella.

'I know, it was a lucky escape!' I agreed.

When Mama was settled in her soft white sheets, with her pretty quilted counterpane tucked around her, Estella drew me into the drawing room to talk.

'I am so shocked, Sophie. Mama looks much aged and quite ashen. What on earth is the matter?'

'We simply do not know, Stella. Even the doctors are baffled,' I explained. 'You already know how the Queen overworks her, and since we brought her home we have been nursing her as best we can. What more can we do to cheer her?'

'I was wondering . . .' Estella said thoughtfully. 'Shall we send for Harry? You know how his antics make her smile. What do you think?' she asked me.

'I did wonder about that,' I mused. 'And why not?'
I decided, feeling the warm family spirit enveloping
me. 'He needs to come back for the wedding in any
case, so we may as well fetch him back a little sooner!'

Estella nodded. 'I shall ask Papa to send a message
to the headmaster at The Glebe. Harry will be
pleased to get out of there and I'm sure he will cheer
Mama up no end.'

I spent the evening quietly. I was tired from the
journey and it was pleasant to walk in the grounds of
the Daisy Park, enjoying the pretty spring garden and
chatting with my sister.

On the Monday morning I realized with delight
that Lucy would soon be arriving with news of the
ball, and as I gathered spring flowers from the walled
garden, a note arrived to say that Lucy and Lady
Lennox were resting at the nearest coaching inn at
Moreton-in-Marsh, and would soon be with us.

My heart sang. It would be wonderful to hear all
about the ball – and whether Lucy had danced with
Mr Hughes.

Chapter Five

As we awaited Lucy and Lady Lennox's arrival, a messenger arrived.

'Ah, Lord Sandford's crest,' observed Estella, examining the envelope. 'My in-laws are staying with him at Mellorbay Hall, remember?'

I nodded. I had met Lord Sandford a few times at local events in Whistling Sparrows. From what I could remember he was tall and handsome in a military way. Three years earlier, when I was fourteen, his young wife had died most tragically in childbirth.

Estella opened the note as we enjoyed a cold luncheon of ham and salad together in the dining room.

'Ah! He is inviting us all to dine with him this evening,' she said. 'He has some young company from the city – recovering from the Queen's ball, by all accounts – as well as Percy and his family, and he wants to make a party of it.'

'But what of Lucy and Lady Lennox? We cannot leave them here alone, with dear Mama poorly in bed!' I pointed out.

'Yes, of course. Hmm. Would it be very rude to ask if they might be included?' pondered my sister.

'As I recall, Lord Sandford is a kindly man who doesn't stand on ceremony. If he has young friends down from London, Lucy will simply love it,' I said, keen that we should all be of the party. 'And could we ask Miss Bowes to sit with Mama, just for the evening? They get along so well.'

'That's a brilliant idea, Sophie!' agreed Estella. 'And I'm sure Lord Sandford won't mind. I will pen him a note right away . . .' And she set about writing to Lord Sandford and Miss Bowes, while I walked to the end of our driveway, hopeful of meeting my best friend as she arrived.

I was not disappointed. As I neared the black wrought-iron gates, a shiny, dark-burgundy coach turned into the drive; a pretty peaches-and-cream face framed by glorious golden hair was hanging out of the window as the coachman reined in the horses.

'Sophie! I'm breathing the country air to make my cheeks pinker. Is it working?' cried Lucy.

'Yes, Lucy, they are very pink indeed!' I called back. 'How lovely to see you! Good afternoon, Lady Lennox.'

'Good afternoon, Sophia. How pretty this place always looks! And how is your dear mother?' enquired Lucy's aunt.

I jumped into their coach for the ride back down to the house. 'She is no worse, thank you, Lady Lennox,' was the best I could say, 'but she's not receiving, as I'm sure you'll understand.'

'Of course, dear. We can only hope to see her stronger in time, that's all,' said Lady Lennox kindly.

Lucy whispered to me, 'We'll go for a walk shortly, and I will tell you everything about the ball!'

Lady Lennox smiled and looked ahead as though she hadn't heard a word.

When we had all taken tea in the drawing room – without Mama, of course – Estella received a second note from Mellorbay Hall.

'Lord Sandford says he would very much like to invite Lucy and Lady Lennox to dinner this evening. There is to be a merry party of twenty or more,' explained Estella. 'Oh, do say you'll come!' she cried, looking at our guests.

Lucy glanced at Lady Lennox for approval, and she nodded happily.

'Hooray!' Lucy whispered to me. 'A party. And hosted by the wealthy Lord Sandford – who is said to be very handsome! I can't wait! Now, let's go into the garden and gather posies for our dresses for this evening,' she suggested with a wink.

We linked arms and made our way through the long orchard as the warm spring sun shone down on us.

'So, Lucy. Tell me all. Did you see him – the Adorable Johnny Hughes?' I asked.

'Oh, Sophie, he was there, but only briefly. I heard he was dancing, and I went to powder my nose so I would be looking my best if I bumped into him, and then, when I returned, I was told he had gone! All night long I hoped to see him return, but alas, he did not. Can you believe what rotten luck that was?' sighed Lucy.

'A missed opportunity indeed,' I agreed. 'How elusive he is! But there will be other occasions to meet him, I'm sure. And there must be other gossip to tell?'

'Of course. Well, you know your neighbour in Mayfair, Arabella de Villeneuve?'

'Yes, of course. Go on – this sounds interesting, Luce,' I said.

'As you know, she has been engaged to Lord Somerset for months, but he has been dilly-dallying and there was no date set for a wedding. Well, in order to make him jealous, she danced all evening with Mr James Pitt, nephew to the former Prime Minister.'

'Hmm. He's not bad looking – if a bit namby-pamby for me,' I commented.

'I agree,' said Lucy. 'Anyway, they say that Lord Somerset was all of a sudden sick with jealousy, and declared that they should marry with the greatest of haste. And do you know what Arabella said? She said "No!" That she has fallen in love with Mr Pitt is certain – and her engagement to Lord Somerset is off!'

'Oh my goodness!' I gasped.

Lucy nodded. 'What started as a ruse to make her fiancé jealous has turned into true love!'

'It is amazing,' I laughed. 'But I say *good for her*. He's kept her dangling for two years or more!'

'I know, and she's already twenty-three!' agreed Lucy.

It was lovely to hear Lucy's news. When we had gathered our posies and returned to the house, I was thrilled to see that my mother was taking tea in the day room with Mrs Willow and Lady Lennox.

'Mama! How lovely to see you up and dressed!' I exclaimed.

'Well, Sophia, we have guests. And I can rest when you all go out to dinner later,' said Mama. She looked fragile, but a little more like herself in a cosy mauve day dress with pretty bows on the bodice.

I was so uplifted by the improvement in my mother's health that I became very excited about the dinner party, and Lucy and I tried to guess who might be there. We asked Estella if she knew.

'There will be the Dovetails and ourselves, of course. Then the Reverend Allen will be there, and Mr Archer, the lawyer from Crossbows House. But there are a few more, seemingly,' she explained – she had been gathering snippets of information from notes she'd been exchanging all day with her fiancé, Mr Dovetail.

'Let's make ourselves look as lovely as possible,' I said to Lucy. 'Shall we go upstairs and try on some dresses?'

'Yes, this party sounds like fun. I've brought jewellery and scarves and hairbands. Come on!' enthused Lucy, who has a great eye for fashion.

We rushed upstairs to the big dressing room, which has a vast gold-framed mirror on a stand.

We laid out all the possible options and I decided on a pale pink dress, with a white posy at the neckline and a simple pearl choker. Lucy settled on a powder blue, low-cut satin gown, with sapphires at her throat and ears. Lucy has far more bust to reveal than I, but I live in hope of developing further in that area. (I have been doing some exercises which are supposed to help. No luck so far!)

Once we had settled on our outfits, we decided to have a bath. Our country housekeeper, Miss Larch, was quite appalled by our 'over-washing', as she called it. 'You'll wash away all the natural oils from your skin and then you'll be needing creams for moisture, I've no doubt,' she told us. 'And who'll be profiting? The cream-makers, that's who!'

Then she remembered herself and said, 'Two baths will be ready in twenty minutes, Miss Musgrove, all scented and what not. One in the middle bathroom and one in the top.' Lucy and I giggled nervously and thanked her. We never know if Miss Larch will be jolly or cross, which puts us on edge a little.

After bathing, we put on our robes as we dried our long hair and smoothed creams into our skin – just as Miss Larch had predicted.

Lily is an absolute wizard with hair-dos. We only have to show her a picture in a French magazine and she looks in her box of pins, nets, curlers, combs and clips, before saying, 'Yes, I'm sure I can do that, miss.' I think she practises on her own hair on her days off.

Once we were dressed in our undergarments and slips, it was time for Lily to weave her magic. She had brought some pretty pearl brooches in her box. I had not thought to pack them for the country, but Lily thinks of everything. She fastened the brooches onto velvet hairbands, which were placed on our up-dos. 'Now then, you're both as pretty as Gainsborough pictures, I must say,' she told us happily. 'A bit of lip cream on your lips and kohl on your eyelashes and you'll steal the heart of any lord!'

As we dithered, changing into different shoes and bracelets, we heard Estella call up from the hallway, 'Girls! We must go. It would never do to be late. What will the Dovetails think of me?'

Hurriedly we emerged, our outfits completed with short jackets which sat at the empire line of the dresses. Mine was made from silky black velvet and Lucy's was in soft ivory duchesse satin. Of course we took pretty reticules too, which Lucy had brought down from London.

'Ta-dah!' said Lucy, posing as we descended the staircase. 'Are you not proud of us, Estella?'

We gazed at Estella, who looked exquisitely pretty in a delphinium silk dress. It had rather too much structure and was a little 'last century', but she still looked gorgeous. Her sweet face, which is heart-shaped with large wide-set eyes and a sweet little upturned nose, lit up. 'You're both quite beautiful, so I shall forgive you for taking so long,' she said. 'Come on now!'

We went to kiss Mama goodbye, and I was glad to see that she was enjoying the company of Miss Bowes.

She smiled proudly at us. 'Girls, you look quite divine,' she said, waving us off and looking so cheerful that I was able to look forward to the evening ahead with a light heart.

We jumped into our coach with our chaperones, and waved to Mama and Miss Bowes, who were watching from the drawing-room window. As we set off, we speculated about the party.

'I wonder who the mystery guests will be? I'm *dying* to find out!' said Lucy.

'Probably Sir Billy Crashing-bore,' I said, using our nickname for tedious dinner companions.

'You never know, Sophie. They might be interesting,' said Lucy, as optimistic as ever. 'It's always worth looking your best, even out in the sticks!'

I laughed and agreed, while Mrs Willow and Lady Lennox tutted and pretended to be shocked.

Chapter Six

We alighted from the coach outside Mellorbay Hall and made our way up the fine stone stairway at the front of the house. It is a magnificent building of cream sandstone, designed by Robert Adam in the classical style. The central staircase at the front is flanked by two symmetrical wings, of at least four floors each. It is elegant and grand, and with lamps glowing at every window it also manages to look inviting – and even a little cosy.

Lucy was most impressed, and she winked at me as we stepped into the main house. Our jackets were taken and we were shown into a smart receiving room where some other guests were already assembled. They all stood to mark our arrival and the men bowed politely.

My eyes danced around the room. I recognized

Estella's intended, Mr Dovetail, and guessed that the preening pair attached to him were his parents. In the far corner the Reverend Allen, the vicar who had replaced the now-retired Reverend Bowes – the father of our Miss Bowes – was holding forth about his gift for writing sermons, nearly pinning some poor young lady to the wall.

I soon learned that she was Leonora Pink, a cousin of Mr Dovetail. She had the appearance of a fancy confection – a marshmallow, perhaps – with creamy skin and frothy blonde hair, and she wore a pale pink dress, in the old style. It has to be said that she suits her surname admirably.

I blushed as I spotted Lord Sandford. I had not seen him for over a year and saw that he was not elderly, as I had remembered, but a handsome man in his thirties – which is old, but not *very* old. I felt so sorry for him – bereaved at such a young age. He was always very friendly, with lovely manners, and I liked him well.

He was talking to two handsome young gentle-men, but he came towards us as we entered and warmly welcomed us to the party.

'Let me introduce everyone,' he said. When he came to his two male companions, Lucy and I were paying particular attention as they were both incredibly dashing.

'This is my great friend, Mr Archer, of Crossbows House in the village,' he told us. Mr Archer was a young, athletic-looking man, with dark wavy hair and a devastating smile. Lucy was most impressed by him, and I could certainly see why.

'To his left,' continued Lord Sandford, 'is my distant cousin, the Honourable Johnny Hughes.'

Johnny Hughes! I could not believe it – and Lucy even coughed in surprise. I stole a glance at Mr Hughes's face and saw that the stories of his good looks were not wrong. He had dark, expressive eyes and chiselled features. He was tall and broad, with a soldier's physique, and he smiled in a friendly way. I thought it was a good thing Lucy and I had taken such care with our appearance.

Very soon, Mr Archer was at our side, amusing us with jokes and tricks.

'Did you know, ladies, that I can make gold out of thin air?' he told us playfully.

'Is that so, Mr Archer? You must be exceedingly rich, in that case!' I retorted.

'Ah! I can make it appear, but as yet, I cannot prevent it from disappearing again!' he explained, and Lucy and I both laughed. Lucy was well entertained and I thought Mr Archer was fun too, but I couldn't help feeling a little mistrustful. He reminded me of a confidence trickster I had once encountered at the county fair.

Mr Hughes and Lord Sandford had been talking to someone else, but they now joined in the merriment.

'And Mr Hughes, can you too produce gold from thin air?' I asked.

'Yes, Miss Musgrove. I was the one who taught it to Mr Archer. And, what's more, I know how to keep hold of it!' he replied with a smile.

'Aha! Then that gives you the edge over Mr Archer,' I laughed.

'Of course, but not just in the production of gold!' he told me.

I smiled at this arch-vanity, which was clearly said in jest. Lord Sandford laughed as Mr Hughes whispered to me: 'Ask Mr Archer his first name!'

I did so, and Mr Archer immediately blushed and said, 'Johnny, I'll kill you for that! I shall never reveal it. It is too silly – a family name, my mother's joke. Just call me Archer, please, ladies!'

This was too intriguing.

'Oh, do tell!' begged Lucy. 'I know – we will suggest names and you can simply confirm or deny them. How does that sound?'

'Very well, but you shall never get it – it is quite unique . . .' he teased.

Lucy began. 'Algernon?'

I tried, 'Macbeth?'

Back to Lucy. 'Jesus?' she asked. At which point the vicar rushed over to join us.

'You are discussing religion . . . ?' he began. We all stifled our giggles. I had forgotten that the vicar has the habit of whistling his words out between his teeth, so that he sounds like a kettle coming to the boil.

'As I was just saying to the lovely Miss Pink, I am in want of a wife this year,' he whistled.

At this terrifying prospect, Mr Archer drew Lucy to one side, engaging in polite chit-chat, leaving Mr Hughes, Lord Sandford and myself to manage the vicar, whose favourable image of himself is rather removed from our vision of him.

Mr Hughes seemed to realize that the vicar was extremely dull, and he very charmingly brought the conversation round to topics which were of more interest to me.

'Have you taken the waters at Bath, Miss Musgrove?' he asked.

'Yes, I loved the bathing – though not so much the drinking of the waters,' I confided.

He laughed. 'And did you enjoy the parties and promenading at the Assembly Rooms?' he asked.

'Yes, indeed, although there was not much to look at,' I replied.

'Ah, but if *you* were promenading, I suspect the onlookers would have found more to please the eye than you did,' he told me gallantly.

Mr Hughes was somewhat hard to fathom – always charming, yet somehow giving little away. At first I felt that he had little interest in making my acquaintance, and yet, as I moved off around the room to join Estella and her future in-laws, I noticed that his gaze seemed to follow me.

The dining hall was wonderfully grand, with gold plates and crystal glasses on a vast mahogany table, all glittering in the light of the shimmering chandeliers. Unfortunately, over dinner I noticed that my soon-to-be brother-in-law, Mr Dovetail, was very full of himself.

He snapped his fingers for a footman to attend him, only to fill the poor man's hands with items from his plate that he did not wish to eat! Estella scolded him gently and he became quite red with irritation.

'Estella, dearest, when I want your opinion, I shall ask for it!' he retorted severely, making my poor sister blush.

The conversation turned to the upcoming wedding and the guests. Mr Dovetail began to tell those of us seated around him of an intriguing old school friend of his called Marcus Stevens. 'He'll be there. You must look out for him. He's an exceptionally clever fellow!' he enthused.

'In what way is he clever, Mr Dovetail?' I asked.

'Why, with money, politics, literature. Whatever he does, he does well,' he explained.

We were distracted by the creak of the dining-room door opening, and there before us stood quite the most adorable child I had ever seen.

'Rose, my darling girl!' said Lord Sandford. 'Were you having nightmares, sweetest?'

'Yes, Papa. I need you to read to me, please,' she lisped sweetly. Without a moment's thought, he scooped her up in his arms, asked her to wish us goodnight and took her upstairs for some fairytales.

When he came back down a little while later, I turned to him, as I was seated to his right. 'Lord Sandford, your daughter is the sweetest little thing. I should love to come and play with her and read stories to her one day.'

'How kind, Miss Musgrove. Rose would like that, I know,' Lord Sandford replied, looking delighted.

I glanced up to find Mr Hughes looking at me in

a quizzical way. 'I still love toys, I'm afraid,' I explained, shrugging my shoulders.

After the meal we played games in the great hall and entertained each other with songs and piano-playing. I thought I would explode with suppressed giggles when the vicar took to the floor and sang a ballad, whistling the words through his teeth. When I glanced at Lucy, I could tell she was having similar trouble. Even Mrs Willow had to bite her lips to control her mirth.

As the evening progressed, I became very uneasy at the behaviour of the Dovetails, who seemed to me to be enjoying the hospitality of the kindly Lord Sandford rather too well. Each time I saw Mrs Dovetail, she was gorging herself on sugar-frosted cherries, spitting out the stones into a bowl held up by a poor maidservant. Meanwhile Mr Dovetail was downing glasses of champagne as though it were cheap ale. And they were both unkind in their opinions – on politics, people and etiquette.

'Ooh, she's a slattern!' said Mrs Dovetail at one point, talking of her poor neighbour, a Mrs Forster. 'She serves sherry with fruitcake. Can you imagine?'

And as for Estella's fiancé, I was sorry to note that his eyes went wherever the most female skin was on show. On one occasion he was talking to Lucy about Italy, while staring fixedly at her magnificent décolletage. She bravely tried to ignore his gaze, which certainly did not meet her eye.

But despite these annoyances, it was a splendid evening and I felt quite intoxicated by it. 'I know! Let's play mimes!' I suggested. 'I'll start!'

Everyone agreed that this was a prime notion, so I prepared myself to act out the title of a play. I thought on my feet, and noticing a galleried balcony above the drawing room, decided on *Romeo and Juliet*. I ran up to the balcony and looked down in lovelorn fashion, my hands clasped together in longing.

'Be careful, Sophia!' called Mrs Willow anxiously. 'You're going to fall over the edge!'

I ignored her and accidentally fixed my gaze on Mr Hughes, who was looking up at me in a heroic manner. Perhaps due to the wine we had been served, I was rather unsteady and I could feel myself spinning a little.

'*Romeo and Juliet!*' he said.

'Hooray!' I cried, luckily falling backwards onto a chair instead of tumbling over the edge of the balcony. (It could have gone either way!) Mr Hughes came running to my rescue and I found myself laughing at my dizziness. I could hear the others carrying on with the mimes below, but the room was spinning slightly around me.

'Are you unused to champagne, Miss Musgrove?' asked Mr Hughes gently.

'Yes. I'm sorry . . .' I laughed.

'Do not be sorry. Let's go out for some air,' he suggested.

I agreed and we made our way out to the terrace. I shivered as a chill wind blew across the park, and then I felt him draping a warm jacket around my shoulders.

'Thank you,' I said.

He smiled. 'It has been a pleasure making your acquaintance this evening, Miss Musgrove. You were not at Queen Charlotte's ball . . .'

'No, sir. I was looking after my mother. Unfortunately she has a mystery illness, which is worrying us all greatly.'

'I am sorry to hear of it,' he said. 'I trust that when we next meet, she will be quite cured. I have recently been invited to the forthcoming family wedding by your sister's fiancé, so I shall be back here soon.'

'Ah! I am excited about the wedding, but not about losing my sweet sister,' I lamented.

'You are close to your sister?' he asked.

'Very close,' I replied. I was quiet for a moment. My family were my whole world. I could not imagine life any other way. I felt a pang of anxiety about my mother's illness and quickly asked Mr Hughes about his siblings.

We were deep in conversation when we were interrupted by the shrill laughter of Lucy, who was still in party mood. 'Ah, Sophie! I last saw you perched on the edge of the balcony. I'm glad you are still alive!' she cried.

'And I'm glad to see that you are still standing on your own two feet,' I laughed.

It was time to go home to the Daisy Park. After we'd requested our jackets, Lord Sandford saw us off as warmly as he had welcomed us. 'It has been a pleasure, Miss Musgrove,' he said. 'And perhaps you would honour us by visiting Rose soon?'

'Of course. I will come tomorrow after lunch, if I may?' I suggested, thinking what a sweet child Rose seemed – and without a mother too. It was too cruel.

Before we got into our coach, Mr Hughes came to say goodnight. His manner was rather stiff and formal, but there seemed to be warmth underneath. 'Until the wedding, Miss Musgrove,' he said.

'Yes, I shall look forward to seeing you there, Mr Hughes,' I replied.

Lady Lennox, Mrs Willow and Estella were waiting for us in our carriage, and we soon set off on the short journey home. But as we travelled down the driveway of Mellorbay Hall, we suddenly heard footsteps running alongside us. Our driver pulled up, and Mr Archer reached in to wish Lucy goodnight. He kissed her hand dramatically before taking his leave.

Later, as we sat in our nightgowns on my chaise, sipping hot milky drinks provided by Miss Larch, Lucy and I talked over the events of the evening.

'I can't believe how exciting it all is, Sophia!' Lucy exclaimed. 'I have a new admirer, *and* we have finally met the Adorable Johnny Hughes!'

'Yes, at last,' I agreed.

'What do you think of him?' Lucy asked.

I smiled. 'He does not disappoint.'

Lucy laughed. 'And consider Mr Archer! I have never felt less disappointed either, Sophie dear. Isn't life fun?'

Chapter Seven

Estella had been notified that our little brother, Harry, would be arriving the next day and we were all up early, listening for hooves and Harry's crazy whoops as he came down the driveway. Mama sat up in bed and allowed Lily to style her hair and apply a little pink rouge, so as not to scare Harry with her pale face.

Lucy chatted all morning about 'her' Mr Archer, and we marvelled at the fact that we had come all the way to rural Whistling Sparrows to finally meet Johnny Hughes.

'You spent ages talking with him, Sophie. Did you like him?' she asked.

'Which one?' I replied.

'Well, Mr Archer, as we know, is heavenly, but I meant Mr Hughes.'

'Hmm. He's rather deep,' I commented.

'Just like you!' retorted Lucy.

Before lunch I was pleased to hear the sound of a carriage approaching. Little Harry Musgrove was back, hotfooting it home from the School for Scamps!

He was sitting up with the driver, jousting with a huge pole of some sort, and prodding it at an imaginary opponent.

'Take that, scoundrel! I'm not afraid of Dick Turpin!' he was shouting.

When he saw Estella, Lucy and me, he began to wave in a crazy fashion.

'The three witches from *Macbeth*! I shall have to kill you all!' he called, before jumping from the carriage and running towards us at top speed. He hugged us all tight as we ruffled his hair and marvelled at how much he had grown, and then Dinky leaped up into his arms, recognizing that his partner-in-crime had returned.

'Where is Mama?' Harry asked. The school had simply been told that it was time for Harry to come home for the wedding, and we had yet to break the news to him that Mama was very poorly.

His little face crumpled when we told him. A friend of his had lost his mother in a fever a few months earlier, so he was full of concern.

'I want to see her!' he said, running into the house. We found him racked with sobs at Mama's feet, with his head on her lap.

She stroked his hair. 'I'll be better soon, Harry,' she told him. 'And I'm all the better for seeing you, my darling.'

That afternoon Miss Bowes sat with Mama again, while Lucy and Lady Lennox went for a walk into the village. I visited little Rose Sandford, as I promised, and we got along famously. Her nurse, Ginny, took a break while I was there, and Rose showed me her nursery. It is heavenly and full of beautiful toys.

When we had tired of all the indoor games, we went to look for butterflies out in the wildflower meadow. She didn't want to catch them, which Harry would have done; she just wanted to look for them, but we didn't have much luck as it was rather early in the year.

'Do you know what my dream is, Miss Musgrove?' she asked me.

'No, Rose, what is it?' I asked.

'To be a fairy princess!' she exclaimed.

'And what does a fairy princess do?' I enquired, thinking back to the days when I loved to hear stories of fairies from Mrs Willow.

'They wear the prettiest dresses and scatter flowers wherever they go,' she explained. My mind began to whirl. This was a dream Estella and I could possibly make come true . . .

'That's a lovely dream, Rose,' was all I said, and we went back to the house to play hide-and-seek.

Rose soon found my hiding place in a toy cupboard in the nursery, and we were laughing and dancing around the room when I suddenly became aware that we were being watched, and blushed as I saw Lord Sandford standing in the doorway.

'Oh, Lord Sandford, I'm sorry – I didn't see you there,' I gasped.

'Do not apologize, Miss Musgrove. It is a charming scene,' he replied with a smile.

That afternoon, during tea at the Daisy Park, I put forward my idea.

'Stella, what would you say if I suggested we invite Rose to be a flower girl at the wedding? I think it would be a dream come true for her,' I explained. (I was to be a bridesmaid, along with Leonora Pink – Mr Dovetail had no sisters; Harry, to his disgust, was to be a pageboy.)

'Sophie, how sweet she would look! I should have thought of it before. I'll ask Lord Sandford, and if the seamstress can come over tomorrow we can have her measured right away!'

'Oh, that's wonderful,' I said. 'She wants to look like a fairy princess – which means she wants the prettiest dress and the chance to scatter flower petals.'

Estella laughed and clapped her hands. 'She'll be perfect!' she declared, and I felt happy at the thought of how excited Rose would be.

The next morning was the day of Lucy's departure. As we sat drinking tea, we were informed by Miss Larch that we had a gentleman caller.

'Oh, my goodness, my eyes are all puffy!' exclaimed Lucy. 'Who is it, Miss Larch?'

'It's Mr Archer from Crossbows House,' she replied.

'Oooh! Show him into the drawing room, please,' I said.

Estella was much amused by Lucy's excitement. My friend immediately insisted on getting some lettuce leaves to bathe her eyes – her beauty almanac said this would make them sparkle – before she went down to meet Mr Archer.

Miss Larch was less entertained by Lucy's beauty requirements when we went to ask for the lettuce. 'I never heard of garnish on a lady's face before!' she exclaimed, handing over the leaves reluctantly. 'What a waste! I was going to make soup with that salad.'

I think Lucy felt that Mr Archer was worth it though, for he was devastatingly charming and regaled us with hilarious stories.

'Lady Lucy . . .' he said falteringly as he stood to take his leave. 'Perhaps we could meet in the city next week? I would very much like to renew our acquaintance.'

'Here is my card,' said Lucy, smiling. 'I should be pleased to see you again.'

After he left, Lucy and I giggled. 'There could be a double wedding with Stella and Mr Dovetail!' I joked, but Mrs Willow tutted and resumed her cross-stitch.

It was hard to see Lucy go home later that day.

'I'll be back in three weeks for the wedding,' she said. She was coming with her chaperone, Lady Lennox. Lady Pennington was about to give birth again, so she and Lord Pennington had politely declined the wedding invitation. I knew it wouldn't be long before Lucy's return, but everything was much more colourful with her around and I was sure I would miss her over the next few weeks.

'Mr Archer *is* invited to the wedding, isn't he, Sophie, dear?' she whispered.

'I promise he'll be there!' I told her.

'He's promised to write to me. And we are to go to a Mozart recital at Carlton House soon. I know I've said it before, but I think he could be The One, I really do, Sophie!' she said.

'We'll see what Lord Pennington makes of his credentials first,' scolded Lady Lennox, chivvying Lucy into the coach.

Mrs Willow, Estella and I waved them off, then went indoors to get on with the wedding arrangements. I was looking forward to the next three weeks of planning. It was exciting and – as it turned out – took up our every waking moment.

Rose Sandford was thrilled when she was asked to be a flower girl. 'I will be a fairy princess at last! Thank you!' she cried, embracing me with her chubby little arms. She was fitted for a dress, and her nurse often brought her over to the Daisy Park to join in the planning. On one occasion her father accompanied her, and it was lovely to see his pride in his little girl.

'You are so natural with children, Miss Musgrove,' he observed, smiling warmly at me. He handed me a small package tied with a ribbon.

I looked at him quizzically.

'It's a small token of my appreciation for all you have done for Rose,' he said.

I opened the package and found inside a pair of exquisite pearl earrings. 'Oh, how lovely!' I gasped. 'Thank you, Lord Sandford. These are so pretty! But, really, you didn't need to—'

'I know. I wanted to,' he said firmly.

We all adored Rose, including Harry, who loved having someone smaller than himself to organize.

We eagerly awaited the arrival of Estella's gown from Paris. It was to be kept a secret from Papa, who came down to the Daisy Park to check on Mama's progress every so often: he hated all things French. When there were only ten days left until the wedding, we became terribly worried that the dress would never arrive at all.

I went down to the village to check if any packages had gone astray, when I saw Lily chatting to Ruth, a maid from Crossbows House. They were deep in conversation and I couldn't help noticing that Lily looked most perturbed. I carried on to the postal office, only to find that they had no lost packages there, but my mind kept wandering back to the worried look on Lily's face.

* * *

That night, as she brushed out my hair, Lily mentioned that she had been chatting to Ruth so I took the opportunity to ask her about it.

'Did you enjoy your conversation, Lily?' I asked.

'Yes, miss,' she replied. 'It's just that . . . Well, you see . . . Oh, never mind.'

'Lily, you know you can tell me anything,' I said, trying to sound reassuring. 'Do you want to talk to me about something?'

'Oh, Miss Sophia. It's regarding Ruth's master, Mr Archer. She says that he's involved in them cruel slave ships in some way!' Lily burst out. 'I didn't know whether to tell you, miss, but I know that Lady Lucy holds him in high regard, and I couldn't bear the thought of her being caught up in anything bad.'

I bit my lip. I knew a little about the slave trade from newspapers and general society gossip. Some families saw nothing bad in it, I knew, but others were appalled by the trade in human beings. I had always heartily disliked the idea of buying and selling people. It seemed to me entirely wrong. Besides, there were rumours that on the ships that brought the slaves into the London docks, they were often tied up and starved during the journey. It was a terrible business and I didn't want to believe that Mr Archer was involved in it in any way.

'You were right to tell me, Lily,' I reassured her. 'And I will think about what and whether to tell Lucy . . .' This information about Mr Archer could well be mistaken. Perhaps Ruth had overheard unkind and unfounded gossip, or had simply misunderstood the complexities of Mr Archer's business dealings. It could even be that for some reason she didn't want her master to court Lucy and was trying to poison our thoughts against him. Would it be right to pass on this gossip when I had no evidence at all?

I had just received a letter from Lucy informing me that Mr Archer was visiting her regularly in London; a chaperoned theatre trip with him had gone wonderfully well. On reflection I decided to say nothing about this news for the time being. I couldn't bear to disturb Lucy's happiness or to blacken the name of a man who might have nothing to do with the slave ships. Still, the unpleasant snippet of gossip preyed on my mind, and it was some hours before I fell asleep that night.

Chapter Eight

With only a week to go until Estella's wedding, I didn't have time to think too much more about Mr Archer. The whole Musgrove family was working hard to give our beloved Estella the day she had always dreamed of. I must confess that I caught the wedding bug a little myself – it was such a wonderful project – but I was determined that I would only ever marry when I had found my true love.

Our excitement was increased when a messenger arrived, bearing an envelope with the distinctive royal seal upon it. We had been waiting to hear if the Queen had accepted our invitation to the wedding.

'Come quickly!' cried Estella. 'We have a letter from the Queen!' No matter how infuriating Queen Charlotte could be, she was still the highest lady in the land, and it would be a great honour if she were to attend Estella's wedding.

We gathered round my mother's bed to hear the news. 'It says that Her Majesty, Queen Charlotte, will be delighted to attend the wedding and that she will be accompanied by her daughter, Princess Amelia,' Estella squealed. 'And they will be staying in the area with friends so that they shall not impose on us at this busy time. How thoughtful!'

'Hurrah!' I cried, hugging Estella.

'The Queen herself!' she breathed as she hugged me back.

'It is wonderful news, Stella, dear,' Mama said happily.

Luck really seemed to be with us when, finally, with only a few days to go, the wedding dress arrived from Paris. It was truly divine, falling in soft silken folds from a high waist, with a lace overlay stitched with pearls covering the entire gown. It even had a slight train behind it that looked very glamorous. This dress was a totally new look which I had seen in a magazine and persuaded Estella to order some months before. It was becoming fashionable to wear a special white wedding dress, instead of simply donning a best gown, and I knew that white would suit Estella's colouring perfectly.

'I love it!' Estella cried.

'It's *so* modish,' I remarked, helping Estella to slip it on. But she must have lost a lot of weight – or sent the wrong measurements to Paris – because the beautiful dress simply fell off her shoulders and hung like a sack.

'Oh, dear, it's much too big!' I declared, stating the obvious.

'What can have gone wrong?' Estella wailed. 'And more to the point, what can we do about it with only a few days to go?'

'Perhaps the seamstress in the village can alter it, dear,' I suggested.

But Estella shook her head. 'I'm afraid not. She's terribly offended that I didn't ask her to make my wedding dress, even though she is making the bridesmaids' dresses and Harry's suit. She predicted that I would regret ordering it from France.'

'Hmm, what a pickle. We don't want Papa to know where it came from – and that it is faulty after all that!' I mused. 'He would be too smug. Fetch me the sewing box – *I* will adjust it!' I declared.

Estella's face crumpled. 'But, Sophie, dearest, you are not known for your sewing skills,' she said as sweetly as her anxious state would allow.

I laughed at this. It was true. I always sewed my cross-stitch samplers to my skirts by accident! 'But I will be careful, I promise,' I assured my sister. 'I will pin it where it hangs loose and take it in a little over the shoulders. We want to show off your pretty curves after all!'

I really did try my best. I took hours over the stitching, and they were the neatest little back stitches you ever saw. Estella came back to my room to try on the dress again, but disaster of all disasters, I had stitched up the armholes during my shoulder alterations!

Estella burst into hysterical laughter as she struggled to push her arms into the dress. She danced around the room with only her head through the neck.

'It's a straitjacket, Sophie! I am finally insane! I am King George, what, what!' she cried, before we both collapsed on my bed in a mixture of laughter and tears.

I ran to fetch Mrs Willow.

'What *is* going on?' she asked loudly.

'Ssshh!' I hushed her. 'It's a secret!'

Three hours later, Mrs Willow had undone my stitches and redone the work with her own. What a lovely job she did! She had made the dress look made-to-measure and it sat perfectly on Estella's dainty frame. We were all quite speechless for a moment as we admired the exquisite bride-to-be.

'Well, you're quite the most beautiful bride I've ever seen,' exclaimed Mrs Willow. 'And if I may so, strictly between these four walls, it was well worth sending to France for this dress. It's magnificent!'

This was praise indeed from Mrs Willow, and Estella glowed with pride.

Harry was a little darling in the days leading up to the wedding, moving awnings and tents around the garden and helping to create the most gorgeous fairy glade in the dell at the bottom of the garden. Estella wanted it to be crammed with lanterns, flowers and drapes.

'A right fire hazard and no mistake!' observed Miss Larch cheerily.

The day before the wedding we received another message with the royal seal. It was addressed to Mama.

'Come quickly, Stella, dear,' she called. She was now having good days and bad days by turns. The good days were enough to keep us from despairing too much over her condition, but the cause of the malaise was still a mystery. 'The note says that the Queen is certain to attend tomorrow. She is at the

Earl of Oxford's country house as we speak, ten miles to the north, along with the Princess Amelia!'

'Hurrah!' we all cried. We had been worried that she would cry off at the last moment, as she was sometimes prone to do.

'Is the King with her?' I asked anxiously.

'Most definitely not!' replied Mama.

I laughed with relief. To cap our pleasure, Lucy and Lady Lennox arrived before dusk, and Lucy amused us all evening with tales of the London parties she had attended.

She and I managed to snatch a private moment on the landing before we retired to bed.

'Have you seen Mr Archer again?' I enquired. I had been worrying about him in odd quiet moments, and found myself musing about the slave trade. I had never given it a great deal of thought before, but now the rumours of barbaric conditions preyed on my mind and I wondered how much was true.

'No, he was unable to attend the Mozart concert due to business commitments,' Lucy answered. 'But he has written often, saying that he cannot wait to see me at the wedding!'

'He clearly enjoys your company, but remember that you hardly know each other,' I told her, mindful of Lily's warnings. 'Maybe you should still think of other suitors too, Lucy,' I said.

'Oh, Sophie, there is no need for me to look else-where. My Mr Archer is simply perfect!' she replied.

On the day before the wedding, Mama put on one of her pretty dresses and we all dined together as a family in the dining room. Harry loved having us all together again, and I felt quite emotional at the thought that this might be the last time we enjoyed a meal 'en famille' in this way.

The next day my father got dressed early and declared: 'This place stinks of lavender water and rose petals, and there are half-dressed ladies at every turn. Come on, Harry. We'll play chequers in the summer house, m'boy! And bring Dinky along too. That dog is going to start thinking like a girl if we're not careful!' And with that, he, Harry and Dinky disappeared into the gardens, not to be seen again for several hours.

I watched as Lottie helped my mother into a pale blue gown, with a matching satin pelisse coat and a large feathered hat, which made her look like an exquisite figurine.

'You are so pretty, Mama!' I declared. 'And you look well. Do you feel well?'

'I feel very well indeed!' she said with a smile;

though I had no way of knowing if this was quite true.

Estella was a picture in her French gown. Leonora Pink and I wore simple white dresses, trimmed with lace. They were rather low cut, and sadly my expansion exercises had miserably failed to improve my bust.

'What about a little assistance?' suggested Lily.

'Whatever do you mean?' I asked, intrigued.

'I've heard of it from the other maids, miss. Some of their young ladies enhance what nature has given them with padding!'

I gasped. 'That would be deceitful!' I exclaimed. Then I added, 'What sort of padding?'

Lily rigged up a little wadding in my undergarments and the effect was remarkable. I decided that a little help in that department would not go amiss.

Harry stared, open-mouthed, when he saw me. 'Ugh. You look horribly grown up, Sophie!' he declared, looking at my décolletage. I laughed, secretly rather pleased with Lily's work. It is much simpler than exercises!

Lucy looked quite stunning in a dove-grey French gown with a matching hairband. Little Rose arrived accompanied by her nursemaid, Ginny. She was already wearing what we called her 'fairy princess dress' of pale blush-pink, with little chiffon 'wings' attached to the back.

The wedding ceremony was to take place in the chapel at Mellorbay Hall. The carriages that were to convey us there drew up at the front entrance of the Daisy Park, all decked out with flowers and ribbons arranged by dear Lily.

I was so proud of all my family and friends, but sore at heart when I thought of how wasted Estella was on the Dovetails. However, perhaps I would never have considered anyone good enough for my beloved sister. 'I do hope Mr Dovetail is kind to her . . .' I sighed.

'Don't worry, Soph,' whispered Harry as he saw a tear spill from my eye, 'I'll protect Stella against Mr Dovetail if he's mean to her!' He patted his pockets and showed me a catapult and a small tin of worms.

I laughed and ruffled his hair as Rose sat on my lap. When we arrived at the chapel, Lord Sandford was waiting and he waved to his daughter proudly. Then he turned to me with a look of what I can only describe as affection. I felt a little alarmed. I hoped that he had not assumed I was seeking out his company when I visited Rose. But these thoughts soon flew from my mind as my attention was taken up with the wedding.

The royal coach was arriving, surrounded by a crowd of people, creating a bit of a scrimmage, which had to be marshalled by some of the young men. I noticed that Mr Hughes swiftly took control of the situation.

The Queen and Princess Amelia, dressed in royal purple and rose pink respectively, descended and waved graciously as they were escorted to their front-row seats in the chapel, along with several ladies-in-waiting.

The church service passed without incident, even though Lucy could not suppress a giggle as the Reverend Allen whistled through the prayers. I noticed that Mr Archer was staring at her throughout the whole service, and in truth they did make an elegant pair when I saw them laughing together outside the church.

'I shall throw my posy over my shoulder now, and whoever catches it will be married next!' said Estella. She turned her back to the crowd and threw her flowers into the air. There was much hilarity when the posy was caught by Mr Archer!

'Well, I couldn't let it drop, now, could I?' he protested.

'Beware! If you get married, Archer, you'll have to say your first name!' called Mr Hughes, which caused Mr Archer to throw the posy at him.

'My sister's bouquet!' I cried, and Mr Hughes salvaged it and tied it back together. He passed it back to me with a little bow and I couldn't help but smile at his gallantry.

By the time we returned to the Daisy Park, a string quartet was playing pretty waltzing music on the lawn, the cake was in place on a table decorated with sugared fruits, and the wedding breakfast – stuffed quail and garden vegetables, followed by scented rice puddings with strawberry sauce – was ready to be served.

After the speeches and the breakfast, I twirled Rose around in the glade by the lake, pretending we were princesses from Fairyland. Lord Sandford caught up with us there.

'Rosie, go and find Ginny. Tell her you must have your face washed. It's all sticky with rice pudding,' he said to his little girl, before kissing her sticky face anyway.

My mouth went dry. I didn't feel comfortable being alone with Lord Sandford, and now here we were, together in the woods, with the music and scents of the party drifting towards us through the trees.

'Miss Musgrove . . . Sophia,' he began. 'I wanted

to thank you for all you have done for Rose. She has seldom been this happy. You have a wonderful way with her.'

I took a step back, keen to restore a respectable distance between us. 'She is adorable, my lord. It has been my pleasure,' I replied, turning to head back to the party.

But Lord Sandford stopped me. 'You see, Sophia,' he went on, a slightly misty look in his eyes, 'you are quite—'

But at that moment he was interrupted by Harry, who came crawling through the woods with a sword held out in front of him.

'Harry, you'll get filthy doing that!' I scolded. 'Do excuse me, Lord Sandford, while I attend to this little rascal. With my mother being so fatigued I must look after him.'

'Why, of course, Miss Musgrove. For one so tender in years, the way in which you deal with responsibilities is commendable,' he concluded.

As Harry and I wandered back to the Daisy Park to find him a clean suit, he turned to me and said: 'Came to your rescue, didn't I, Soph?'

'Yes, Harry, you darling little monster, I rather think you did,' I told him.

He chased me indoors with a worm in his hand.

When I returned to the party, I noticed that the lake, which had six little rowing boats upon it, had become the centre of activities. As dusk fell, some of the young gentlemen had thrown off their jackets, rolled up their sleeves and set off on races across the lake. Lucy stood on the edge of the water, shrieking encouragement to Mr Archer as he paddled furiously in his bid to impress her. Mr Hughes was in another boat, and rowed his way across the finishing line in first place, looking quite unruffled.

There was dancing too – mainly cotillions – and the lanterns gave the wildflower garden a magical, fairytale quality. After the boating contest, I noticed that Lucy and Mr Archer were dancing together time after time, even though Lady Lennox tried to put a stop to it. She isn't really quite firm enough to chaperone Lucy properly – which suits Lucy perfectly.

My thoughts turned again to what Ruth had said about Mr Archer: I so hoped she was wrong, but I found myself worrying about his supposed involvement with the slave ships.

However, it was my sister's wedding day, so I tried to put sad thoughts from my mind as I sat on a rose-pink velvet chair at the edge of the garden and observed the dancers.

I spotted Mr Hughes looking awkward on one side of the dance floor, clearly being pursued by Leonora Pink. I think she was seeking his attention, for she suddenly took a theatrical dizzy turn in front of him, collapsing towards him for support. He steadied her politely and guided her to a chair, where she took out her smelling salts. Mrs Dovetail immediately fussed over her and Mr Hughes withdrew. Seeing me watching, he came over and knelt down beside me.

'Miss Musgrove, how charming you look today,' he said.

'Thank you, Mr Hughes. Have you enjoyed the celebrations?' I asked.

'Yes. This has been the finest wedding I have attended all season,' he replied. 'Would you care to dance, Miss Musgrove?'

'That would be very agreeable,' I said, and he led me onto the dance floor. After the cotillion, with Mr Hughes guiding me around the garden quite securely, my new brother-in-law approached and asked me to dance. I smiled and agreed, of course, though I was rather disappointed that Mr Hughes and I had been interrupted, as he is a fine dancer and very easy company too.

'Perhaps we will have time to converse again later?'

Mr Hughes said as I was led away by Mr Dovetail.

'I hope so, Mr Hughes – if you can catch me!' I laughed.

A few minutes later, as I danced with Mr Dovetail, I caught sight of him helping my mother towards the house. He held her hand and waist supportively and she seemed to me to be in very safe hands, but I made a mental note to check on her as soon as I had a spare moment. Her health had generally been better recently, but she still tired easily.

After several more dances – and a quick visit to Mama's room, where I found her comfortably settled – I headed for the vast crystal bowl of punch, which looked extremely refreshing, with fruit and mint leaves floating in it. As I sipped my drink, I suddenly spotted Lord Sandford making a beeline for me. His eyes had that misty look in them again, and I felt anxious to avoid an awkward conversation. I needed to appear occupied, so I quickly turned to the guest nearest to me and said, 'I do hope you have enjoyed my sister's wedding?'

A devastatingly handsome young man – tall, with blond hair and dancing blue eyes – replied, 'It has been very agreeable, thank you.'

'Oh, I am glad. And was there anything in particular that you liked?' I went on desperately, partly fascinated by his staggering good looks, and partly keen to keep him talking until Lord Sandford had gone.

His eyes sparkled. 'Well, I have been bewitched by *you* today, and that is something that has never happened to me before,' he said conversationally.

'I – I shall take that as a compliment,' I stammered, quite taken aback by this declaration.

'Do please excuse me,' he went on, smiling at my confusion. 'I have not yet introduced myself. I am Marcus Stevens.'

'How do you do, Mr Stevens?' I replied, vaguely recognizing the name. I was sure Mr Dovetail had mentioned him as some sort of genius. 'I am Sophia Musgrove.'

'I am delighted to meet you, Miss Musgrove,' replied Mr Stevens, and with the fragrant spring air, the punch, and the soothing voice of my new companion, I began to enjoy myself immensely.

My peace was soon shattered by the sound of Harry shouting.

'Help!' he wailed. 'I'm stuck!' We looked up to see that he had climbed into a tall sycamore tree without thinking of his route back to the ground.

'Oh, Harry!' I exclaimed. 'How on earth are we going to get you down?'

'I don't know, but think of something, Soph. I'm feeling dizzy up here!' he replied.

In an instant, Mr Stevens had taken off his jacket and was swinging himself up into the tree. He soon reached the branch where Harry was sitting and helped him down, one branch at a time. After an agonizing few minutes they were both back on solid ground again.

'Thank you so much, Mr Stevens!' I said gratefully, clutching Harry to me.

'Don't mention it,' he said. 'I got myself into many similar scrapes at his age.'

'What do you say, Harry?' I demanded.

'Thank you very much, sir,' said Harry dutifully. 'And don't tell anyone I got scared, will you?' he added.

'Your secret's safe with me, Harry,' said Mr Stevens solemnly, shaking his hand, man to man.

Harry ran off happily and I found myself quite falling under the spell of the magnificent Mr Stevens as he chatted easily to me. I didn't notice Lord Sandford's retreat, but when I looked about me, he was gone. I would have liked to speak to Mr Stevens for longer, but we were interrupted by the news that the Queen and Princess Amelia were departing.

Mr Stevens did not leave my side as we waved off the

royal carriage. 'Miss Musgrove, it is rare to converse with such a uniquely intelligent creature as yourself,' he said as the party began to dwindle and his own carriage arrived. 'May I call on you in town during the next few weeks to continue our conversation?'

'That would be quite acceptable,' I said with a cautious smile, not wishing to give away just how much I had enjoyed his company. I handed him a card for Musgrove House. As I watched him climb into his carriage, I couldn't help noticing his athletic build. He looked at me for one long moment as he closed the door, and I felt as though I might melt under the intensity of his gaze.

And so it was that Lucy and I were equally starry-eyed as we fell into our beds that night. I didn't tell Lucy about Mr Stevens. He was as handsome as a Greek god, intelligent as a philosopher – and my secret for now. He was somehow different from everyone else in my circle. And when I pictured him climbing the tree to save Harry, I felt a tingle of excitement run down my spine. I lay awake for a long time thinking of him. For all I knew, I would probably never hear from him again – but how I hoped that I would!

Chapter Nine

The next few days were filled with goodbyes. Harry went back to school, Estella went 'home' to Dovetail Hall, and Lucy and Lady Lennox returned to London, as did Papa. I decided to stay with Mama for a while as she was so sad at seeing Estella married into a new family. Her doctor insisted on more bed rest for her.

I still enjoyed having Rose over to play, but I tried to avoid Lord Sandford. I definitely did not want my motives to be mis-read again.

After a couple of weeks I began to long for the city and my dear friend Lucy, but I was reluctant to leave Mama, and I didn't think she was yet well enough to undertake the journey again.

But it was as if my dear mother could read my mind. 'Why don't you go back up to London, darling?' she suggested one morning as we sat together quietly in her room.

'Won't you be lonely here?' I asked. 'Who will look after you?'

'There are plenty of local ladies to rally round me, especially Miss Bowes, and I have Lottie,' Mama replied. 'Go on,' she urged. 'It will do you good to get back to the city.'

After a few days I agreed to go up to London to conclude the Season.

'I hear from our Miss Larch that Lord Sandford has headed up there for a week or more. Perhaps he will visit you?' Mama said.

I could not lie to my mother. 'Mama, I am not enamoured of Lord Sandford,' I told her. 'I am very sorry if I have given the wrong impression. It was not my intention. I love little Rose, but . . .'

My mother smiled. 'Ah! Perhaps you like Mr Hughes? He *is* very handsome – and I think he likes you too, darling.'

'What makes you say that?' I asked.

'Well, I know he is gallant, but he came to my aid at the wedding just to please you, didn't he?' replied Mama.

'Actually, he is naturally very chivalrous, Mama. I am surprised that you are so cynical,' I teased.

'Ah! Defending him now! So it is Mr Hughes!'

I decided to go along with my mother's assumptions as they seemed to please her.

Mrs Willow, Lily, Dinky and I set off for London two days later. I had mixed feelings about the changes that had happened over the last few weeks. I felt that in a very short period of time, I had changed greatly. I seemed to be approaching the world from a different perspective, and I looked back on my old self, thinking I'd been just a silly child.

I compared myself to Lily and worried about her situation, her income and prospects. She had a hard life, as did so many others. I thought about slavery: was Lucy involved with a man who condoned such cruelties? I wondered. I prayed that Mr Archer was of sound character.

We arrived in Mayfair tired and hot, and went straight to our rooms to freshen up. Then I went down to find my father. He was in his study.

'Papa, how nice to see you,' I said, realizing that I had missed him.

'Sophia, darling, I am delighted to have you back. How is Mama?'

We discussed her health, and then chatted about the wedding.

'Did you enjoy it, darling?' my father asked.

'Yes, Papa. It was lovely. I only hope that dear Estella is happy in her match,' I replied.

'Yes, I hope so too,' he agreed. 'You looked as pretty as pictures, both of you. In fact, I know of at least one gentleman who thinks you are especially beautiful!'

'Really? Do tell!' I said, playing along.

'Why, none other than Lord Sandford himself,' he replied triumphantly.

My heart sank. Why was everyone asking me about him all of a sudden?

'Sophia, the day after the wedding his lordship paid me a visit and asked for your hand in marriage. Of course, I said yes, if it was your wish. And from what I saw when I was at the Daisy Park, I was quite sure that it must be your wish. Is this not exciting, darling? To be the mistress of such lovely houses? He's a fine man, from a very distinguished family.'

I was so horrified that I let out a cry. 'Papa, I am sorry to disappoint you. I can only assume that I have misled Lord Sandford through my interest in little Rose, but I am not ready for a husband, and especially not for one of his great age!'

Papa's face fell. I hated to let him down, but what else could I do? I often found myself thinking of Mr

Stevens – though when I thought of him privately I always called him Marcus – and I knew it would be dishonest of me to encourage Lord Sandford further. Thankfully, it would be easier to avoid him in the wider society of London than in the tiny world of Whistling Sparrows and the Daisy Park.

'Well then,' said Papa, 'I shall write to him and say that the time is not yet right. We'll see how you feel in a while – how's that?'

'That sounds like a good idea, Papa,' I agreed, dreading any return to this subject, but grateful for a reprieve.

'And, Sophia, don't forget to practise your music and embroidery. Such skills are important for a young lady.'

'Of course, Papa,' I replied, resolving to work harder at my needlework – at which, in truth, I had never excelled.

Mrs Willow entered as I slipped out into the hall-way to read through my letters. I was hoping for a message from Marcus amongst the vast pile of mail awaiting me. As I flicked through, looking for any unfamiliar handwriting, I overheard some snippets of conversation between my father and my chaperone.

'Mrs Willow, she's changed so much. I don't

recognize my girl. She's so headstrong and doesn't attend to my views as she once did.'

'I know, but don't worry. It is usual for a girl of her age to rebel a little, Lord Musgrove. She's the same lovely girl as ever she was,' replied Mrs Willow reassuringly.

'Hmm. Estella was not like this, but I dare say you are right. Still, I miss the little Sophia who used to sit on my knee. And as for making Lord Sandford wait – well, the nerve of her! It's almost impressive!' said Papa.

I didn't hear Mrs Willow's reply as someone knocked at the front door at this point.

Hawkes opened the door to reveal a messenger. 'I have a letter here for Lord Musgrove. It is most urgent,' he said. 'It has come all the way from Whistling Sparrows near Cheltenham.'

My heart started to race and beads of perspiration broke out on my forehead. *Mama! It must be bad news about Mama!* I thought. 'Papa!' I screamed. 'A message from the Daisy Park!'

Chapter Ten

*P*apa burst into the hallway with a look of terror on his face. He grabbed the note from Hawkes and tore it open. I tried to read his face as his lips moved almost silently over the words. His expression became altered but I could not decipher it.

'Papa!' I implored at last. '*Do* tell us what it says!'

Mrs Willow placed her arm around me, looking just as worried as I was.

My father scratched his head and a shadow of a smile came over his features. Then he shook his head and muttered, 'Well, I never . . .'

'Papa!' I cried, almost overcome with curiosity and apprehension.

'I'm sorry, Sophia, my dear. Mrs Willow, Sophie, please come into the withdrawing room,' he said. Clearly he didn't want the servants to hear the contents of the message.

Mrs Willow and I huddled together on a sofa for comfort, while Papa stood before us and drew himself up to his full height.

'Your mother's condition has at last been diagnosed,' he said. 'But I'm afraid that the worry is not over quite yet. You see, your mother, my dear Sophie, is with child. The baby is due in about three months, and your mother will need the most tender care before, during and after the event.'

I gasped. 'Mama . . . A baby!' I said disbelievingly. I knew how dangerous childbirth was at any age, but my mother was now forty-two. Still, at least we knew what had been causing her nausea and exhaustion. I wept a little with surprise and relief. Mrs Willow held me in her arms and my father patted my head.

'It is an explanation. But now we must get her safely through the delivery,' he said. 'Should we bring her to London, or send the finest surgeon out to the country?' he pondered aloud.

'Don't move her!' advised Mrs Willow. 'She should stay put until the child is born. Oh, I am so pleased to hear of this! An explanation for the suffering – and another infant to cuddle. How delightful!'

Papa nodded thoughtfully, then frowned. 'I have some work to do,' he said. 'I will bid you both goodnight.' This was typical of him. Whenever he had experienced a shock, he liked to be alone.

A few days later, I was asked to receive a guest. 'Who is it?' I asked Hawkes.

He looked at the calling card. 'It's a Mr Stevens, miss.'

I was suddenly excited and a little nervous all at once. I was delighted that he had come to call on me but anxious to make a good impression. I smoothed my hair, pinched my cheeks to bring a bit of colour into them and took a deep breath before making my way to the receiving room. Mrs Willow bustled along too, of course.

'Mr Stevens, how are you?' I said as I entered. He rose to his feet and greeted Mrs Willow and me quite beautifully. Then we all sat comfortably in front of the fire, where we were served tea and fruited teacakes.

'What do you do for your amusement in the city, Mr Stevens?' I enquired.

He smiled. 'A little politics and a little charity work. Then some cards or boxing of an evening,' he told me.

'Ah! Politics. My father is a member of Parliament,' I told him.

'Oh, really? Do you hold any good causes close to

your heart, Miss Musgrove? The plight of orphans, or the mistreatment of slaves, perhaps?' he asked.

I was immediately reminded of Lily's gossip about Mr Archer and the slave ships. I tried to remember what I had heard of the slave trade, but I felt horribly ignorant at that moment. Hitherto, all I had really cared about were hairstyles and French fashions.

'I am concerned about such problems, certainly,' I replied slowly. 'I would like to know more about them, but Papa does not discuss politics with ladies.'

'I understand. Many gentlemen consider ladies unable to follow the intricacies of political debate, but I have always found the fairer sex to be just as able as any of us men,' he said, smiling at me.

'I agree wholeheartedly,' I said fervently. 'Besides, these issues affect us all,' I added.

'Indeed,' Mr Stevens agreed, looking more serious. 'I am most disturbed by the cruelty of slavery. The trading of people who happen to have a darker skin than ourselves is one of the practices I actively oppose.'

He was voicing an opinion that I had shared ever since the gossip about Mr Archer had prompted me to start thinking about the slave trade for myself. I would have liked to discuss it further, but at this point Mrs Willow cleared her throat anxiously and Mr Stevens promptly changed the subject. We spoke about Estella and Mr Dovetail and the glorious occasion of their wedding.

'It was a lovely day, indeed,' said Mr Stevens. 'I didn't think I'd ever see anyone brave enough to take on old Percy Dovetail. The luck's all his!'

Mrs Willow and I laughed. Of course, we completely agreed that in marrying our lovely Estella Mr Dovetail had got the best of the deal.

As Mr Stevens rose to leave, I felt a sudden pang of anxiety at the thought that I might not see him again, but he soon set my mind at rest.

'Do you enjoy the chocolate shop in Mayfair, Miss Musgrove?' he enquired.

'It is one of my favourite places,' I replied.

'Mine too. In fact, I shall be there next Tuesday from eleven,' he told me.

I smiled, reassured that he wanted to see me again, and he turned to say his goodbyes to Mrs Willow.

As we moved towards the door, I caught my skirts and accidentally knocked into Mr Stevens, dropping my fan. He promptly apologized, though the fault was mine, and as we both bent to retrieve the fan his blue eyes danced and he added with a smile, 'With luck we may bump into each other again soon . . .'

* * *

I couldn't wait for our next rendezvous. I was forever thinking about everything Marcus and I had discussed and I was curious to learn more about slavery. I told Lucy all about him in a letter.

She soon replied:

I recall him from the wedding, and he is a dream to look at, I must admit. I cannot wait to meet him properly. I am quite smitten with Mr Archer, Sophie. We are forever in each other's company these days and I don't know how I lived before I met him!

I persuaded Mrs Willow to set off early from Musgrove House on the Tuesday as I wanted to look at baby clothes before going to the Maison du Chocolat. There were the most adorable little garments in Bennets baby outfitters and drapers, as well as beautiful baby carriages, shawls and bedding. We browsed in there for half an hour or more and I opened an account in my father's name as I fancied we'd be going there often from now on.

'We will have some things sent down to Mama,' I said, 'for there is nowhere fancy like this in Whistling Sparrows.'

Mrs Willow pursed her lips. 'Bad luck to buy before the baby's delivered, Sophie,' she said. 'But we will come back here as soon as the new little Musgrove has hatched.'

I laughed at her turn of phrase.

As eleven o'clock approached, I suggested to Mrs Willow that we treat ourselves to a cup of hot chocolate and a slice of all-butter shortbread at the chocolate shop.

'Oh, what a lovely idea, Sophie,' she replied agreeably. If she recalled that Mr Stevens had said he would be in there at this time she did not mention it, and I felt relieved that things were going so smoothly to plan.

My heart started to beat faster as we entered the delicious-smelling Maison du Chocolat. I tried to glance around the shop without appearing to do so. I didn't want Marcus to think I was too keen. At first I could not spot him, but then my eyes found him sitting by a window, reading a newspaper. And, what luck! There was Mrs Willow's best friend, Mrs Davenport, sitting in a booth with her charge, little Lady Marina – who was ten years of age and a bit of a brat.

'Oh, Mrs Willow. See who it is!' I exclaimed as we were shown to a table and took our seats.

Once Mrs Willow had taken off her hat and coat, she hurried over to greet her friend. And a moment later, Marcus came to join me at our table. Though we sat in the middle of a bustling chocolate shop, I revelled in this privacy – of a kind – at last!

'Miss Musgrove, how nice it is to see you again,' he said with a bow. 'And you are even lovelier than I remembered – if that is possible.' As he spoke, I noticed that his blue eyes sparkled.

I blushed, but I was anxious to show him that I was not merely a vain female but also possessed of a good brain and a desire to use it. 'I have been thinking about our previous conversation,' I told him. 'I am anxious to learn more about the slave trade, Mr Stevens. Perhaps you could educate me?'

'Me?' he said with a smile. 'But I fear I would bore you,' he protested.

'No, really. I would like to know,' I insisted. 'And I have no one to talk to me of such things.'

He nodded and looked thoughtful at this. 'Well, it is a brutal and barbaric practice, I'm afraid,' he said seriously. 'These people are shackled and chained on filthy ships, and many die during the terrible crossings from Africa. Those who survive the journey do not arrive to a pleasant life. I have heard of a "gentleman" who played a game of cards with his slave as the prize money! Can you imagine the humiliation of such a thing?'

I shook my head. 'It is unthinkable,' I agreed.

'I believe it is evil to judge people by the colour of their skin, Miss Musgrove, or by the misfortune of their birth. It makes me ill with shame that we treat these people in such a way,' Mr Stevens said, looking grave. 'But let us change the subject. This is all too sad and depressing.'

'No, it is interesting,' I protested, feeling myself awakening to a horror right here in my own city, on my very doorstep.

At my insistence, Mr Stevens carried on. 'As we sit here today, there are boats docking at East India Quay, full of innocent men and women who have been chained up, beaten and starved. They endure unspeakable hardships, Miss Musgrove. It is a disgraceful way to treat fellow humans.'

I nodded. 'I could not agree with you more. It is vile to treat others with cruelty.'

'You are a remarkable young woman, with the same beauty on the inside that is so apparent on the outside,' Mr Stevens said. 'Just remember, when you consider the horrors of slavery, that there is no need for you to be controlled by the men in society. You can think for yourself and make sure your voice is heard.'

I was gazing into his deep blue eyes and hanging on his every word when, all of a sudden, Lucy came into the chocolate shop, accompanied by Lady Lennox and Mr Archer.

'Hello! I say, Sophie, what a lovely coincidence that we should all be here at the same time. May we join you? And won't you introduce us?' Lucy winked at me and I could tell that she was delighted to have the opportunity to finally meet Mr Stevens. I introduced everyone and for the next few minutes we chatted about society gossip and mutual friends.

I was hoping for some more private conversation with Mr Stevens, but as Lucy, Lady Lennox and Mr Archer rose to leave, Mrs Willow returned to my side and Mr Stevens immediately leaped up and excused himself. I said goodbye to him rather reluctantly and then dreamily sipped on my creamy hot chocolate for the next half-hour – after which Mrs Willow and I made our way to the coach stand in Piccadilly, where our driver, Matthew, was waiting for us.

I was desperate to ask Papa what he thought about the slave trade. I had never heard him discuss it, even though I knew he must deal with such matters all the time at Westminster. I must confess that I had always been rather bored by his work in the past, but recent events had made me determined to take more of an interest.

At dinner that evening I quizzed Papa on the subject, but he was not keen to talk about it.

'Sophie,' he sighed, 'how will we ever marry you well if you turn down the offers of fine gentlemen and then persist in engaging in topics of conversation entirely unsuitable for a young lady of your birth? What am I to do with you? Many fathers would enforce a marriage to the likes of Sandford. He has written to me to say that he is happy to wait for you to mature a little. He is very smitten, my dear. Now, enough of this political talk. You don't understand how complicated it all is.'

I stood up, furious that he was so quick to dismiss my interest in politics. 'Papa, I was wrong to let you give Lord Sandford false hope,' I said firmly. 'I shall never marry him. And I shall not abandon my interest in the slave trade. Have you something to hide that you will not discuss this with me?'

Mrs Willow cast her eyes downwards, not knowing where to look, but I could not be submissive any longer. Mr Stevens had shown me that I was a person in my own right and that not everyone disapproved of a woman who could think for herself. My father wanted to control me, but I had changed.

'Sophia Musgrove, go to your room! You are becoming most unladylike and I have a duty to stifle these changes in you before you turn into a wanton radical whom no decent man will marry!'

I sped from the room, happy to get away. Only Marcus understood my thoughts and feelings, it seemed. Papa simply thought my concerns over the slave trade 'unsuitable'.

I realized that my family life was changing in ways I did not like. Estella was married and gone, my mother was far away at the Daisy Park, struggling through her confinement, and though my father had not changed, perhaps, I found I did not admire him as I once had. How could I respect this man who insisted on shielding me from the realities of the world? And, worse, what if he was one of the terrible men who encouraged slavery? I could not bear it if that were the case. As I lay on my bed, thinking, I resolved to find out more about a subject that now consumed all my thoughts – along with the hand-some and fascinating Marcus Stevens.

Chapter Eleven

My moods were very changeable over the next days, but I was hugely cheered when a note arrived from Marcus.

My dear Miss Musgrove,

I hope this finds you well. I am as bewitched by you as ever and torture myself that you will fall for the charms of another gentleman, but I can only hope that no one will claim your heart.

Your remarkable intelligence and our recent conversation has moved me to let you know about a very informative meeting to be held in Clerkenwell next week regarding the evils of the slave trade. I have written the details below. I would be there to escort you, and can only add that it would be an honour if you wished to join me.

With warmest wishes,
Marcus Stevens

I wrote back immediately.

Dear Mr Stevens
Thank you for your letter. I would be most interested to attend the meeting. You have changed the way I think about the world in general and our society in particular. I am very much looking forward to seeing you there,

Sophia Musgrove

I knew Lucy was still at the Penningtons' London home, so Mrs Willow and I dropped in on her one morning shortly before the meeting.

'Sophia Musgrove!' she exclaimed as soon as we were seated in a private corner. 'You're in love!'

I blushed.

'Is it Mr Stevens?' she demanded.

I confessed to Lucy that I was indeed falling under the spell of Marcus Stevens.

'Ooh, I knew it!' she declared. 'I saw the way you were gazing at him in the chocolate shop. Now, tell me all. I tell *you* everything!'

This was quite true. She wrote to me often about her growing romance with Mr Archer. (She still didn't know his first name!)

'Lucy, if you stop talking for a moment, I promise I will tell you all about him,' I said, laughing.

Her face was a picture of excitement and confusion as I told her how I felt.

'Sophie, he might be risky!' she said at last. 'He is not much seen on the social circuit. All we know of him is what Mr Dovetail said – and can we trust Mr Dovetail's judgement?'

'Lucy, Mr Stevens doesn't do this silly Season thing. He's a thinker, an intellectual,' I explained.

'Ooh, la-di-dah!' giggled Lucy. 'Are you trying to say I won't understand him? Just you watch those clever types, Sophia Musgrove. They're cunning!'

But there was nothing anyone could say to me to put me off Marcus Stevens. I worshipped him.

I am not proud of myself for the way in which I eventually got over to Clerkenwell for the meeting. We had a brand-new trainee coachman called Sid. He had a cheeky look about him, which was what gave me the idea: in exchange for a case of ale from our cellar he agreed to take me over to the meeting and wait for me for the homeward trip.

I had never tried to bribe our staff before – but what was a little underhandedness when I was joining the fight against a huge social injustice? I wasn't hurting anyone, and I certainly did not want to let Marcus down.

As I sat in the meeting, which was held in the salon of Lady Arniston, by all accounts a famous social campaigner, I felt terribly ignorant again. I had little knowledge of the details discussed, which made me feel dim and dull. I took notes to make myself appear more earnest, but at least I was not faking my disgust at the slave trade as they described the details.

I was deeply touched by what I heard that night. When Lady Arniston held aloft branding irons and thumbscrews, as well as jaw openers and hand irons, I was aghast. She said that such devices of torture were regularly used to control the slaves on the journeys from their native countries. I wept at that.

'And now, turning to the march,' said Marcus, 'we need you all to support the powerless and give of your time at the protest march through the City of London . . .'

It transpired that in a few weeks' time a whole group of people were planning to march through the streets of Westminster in protest against the slave trade. Marcus explained where to meet and instructed everyone to wear grey or brown so as not to outshine the message that would be painted on white banners.

'Before we end the meeting,' he concluded, 'I would like to introduce you all to a new member – Miss Sophia Musgrove, daughter of Lord Musgrove, the famous politician.' All eyes turned to me with interest. 'Miss Musgrove, will you accompany us on our protest march next month?' he asked.

'Er, I hope so . . . unless I am away in the country,' I stammered, wondering how on earth I could do anything so radical with a chaperone such as Mrs Willow watching over me.

After the meeting Marcus accompanied me to my carriage. 'Goodbye, Miss Musgrove,' he said. 'I hope I will see you at the march.'

'Yes, I hope so too,' I replied, and with a smile and a bow Marcus went back inside.

'You're taking risks, miss,' said Sid. 'We both are. And I don't know which one of us would be in more trouble if we got found out!'

'I'm sorry to put you in this position,' I replied. 'Am I to take it that you would not do this for me again?'

'Well, I didn't say that exactly,' Sid said thoughtfully. 'You've got to be careful, that's what I mean.' And I was glad he had not said no, because I thought I might well have need of his secret help again before too long.

Marcus had mentioned that there was to be an important debate in Parliament the next morning: it related to the proposed bill to end slavery. I desperately wanted to attend.

'Mrs Willow, I think we shall go to the Palace of Westminster today to hear Papa's cronies debating,' I said after breakfast.

'Does your father know of this idea of yours?' she asked.

'No, but it is important that I am educated in these matters, Mrs Willow, if only so that I can understand him better,' I said.

Poor Mrs Willow looked very worried. 'Your father will not approve,' she sighed. 'But come along and let's get this over with. Just you wait until you see how dull it all is.'

I was very excited as we took our seats in the public gallery and I spotted Marcus across the aisle. He looked impossibly handsome as he nodded to me politely.

Suddenly I felt someone sit down beside me and I looked round to find it was Mr Hughes.

'Miss Musgrove, how are you?' he asked.

'I am well, thank you, Mr Hughes,' I replied.

'What brings you here?' he enquired.

'My interest in the debate topic. I am against the slave trade,' I explained.

'We are all against it, Miss Musgrove, but it is how to end it that we must debate,' he said solemnly.

At this point, Marcus looked over and gave me a look which seemed to me to say, *Why are you talking to him?*

Mr Hughes must have seen the look, for he said, 'Be careful who you mix with. These are dangerous subjects – ruthless people abound, Miss Musgrove. Do promise me you will be careful.'

'I will be careful, but not cowardly,' I said pointedly.

During the debate, which put Mrs Willow into a sound sleep, my father himself spoke about the need for heavier fines on ships' captains who illegally and inhumanely transported slaves. I was proud of him and greatly relieved, for I took this to mean that he was fighting the good fight after all. Mrs Willow woke at the end and looked as if she thought she had made the right decision in allowing me to come when she saw me applauding Papa's words enthusiastically.

Afterwards, Mr Hughes asked if Mrs Willow and I would join him for coffee to discuss the debate. I saw that Marcus had left and Mrs Willow looked keen, so I agreed. I wanted to be educated in politics. There were whole gaps in my knowledge, which I found very frustrating, and I thought that perhaps Mr Hughes could fill in some of those gaps.

He found us a table in a lovely new refreshment house, called Harvey's, near the Thames.

'How is your mother?' he asked as we sat down at a table laid with a pure white cloth and shiny silverware.

'Well, not better, but we do know what is causing her to feel unwell,' I said.

'Oh?' he responded.

'She is expecting a baby!' I declared proudly.

'How very exciting. Please convey my best wishes to her, Miss Musgrove. She is a very fine lady.'

'Yes, she is, and thank you, I will do so in my next note to her,' I replied.

'When did you become interested in social problems, Miss Musgrove?' he asked, after ordering us all vanilla coffee creams and walnut cake.

'Just lately. In fact, I have been invited to go on a march next month, which I am considering,' I told him. I suspected that he would disapprove, but I felt the need to assert my independence. It was as if he represented the same type of man as my father. In my view, they both held frustratingly traditional views, thinking that women needed to be protected from the outside world and were unable to make their own decisions – so different from my forward-thinking Marcus Stevens.

But Mrs Willow's face was turning purple. 'Her father is much against this phase,' she chipped in.

'It is not a phase, Mrs Willow. It is my new life,' I informed her.

'Miss Musgrove, it is commendable to have such a fine conscience,' said Mr Hughes. 'You are a credit to your family. But please believe me when I say that I have some experience in the area of activism. My mother and sister have campaigned against poverty for many years, and they have been ill-used by some of the people you might mix with on a march. They have been placed in danger and their money has been appropriated for illegal purposes. I would beg of you not to attend this or any other such event.'

'It is very kind of you to give me your advice, Mr Hughes,' I said haughtily, 'but I will make my own decisions, thank you.' I was becoming annoyed with the way everyone was trying to influence me these days: my father, Lord Sandford, and now Mr

Hughes. Marcus was the one person who actually seemed to respect my real self and I felt lucky to have met him.

Mr Hughes looked amused by my frosty manner. 'Perhaps I might call upon you to see how you fare in the world of politics?' he said, with a slightly mocking smile.

'Or perhaps not!' I snapped. 'Come, Mrs Willow, let us see if there is any word of Mama in the mail at home! Thank you for the coffee and cake, Mr Hughes, it was most refreshing.'

He stood up awkwardly as I rose, and I heard him say, 'Do remember me to your mother, Miss Musgrove . . .' as I swept out of the coffee house.

Chapter Twelve

Mrs Willow was most put out by our speedy departure – she had not quite finished her walnut cake. Besides, she was furious with me for behaving in such a high-handed manner with such an eligible young man. 'Goodness me, Sophie, we're meant to be cultivating good relations with men such as Mr Hughes, not quarrelling with them!' she declared as we took tea together at home later on.

I ignored her. Even Lily had been interfering. She'd told me that Mr Hughes was lovely and that she'd stand on her head to have him look at her just once.

I had laughed. 'Lily, he's actually quite dull – not at all outrageous or daring!'

'Whoever wants "daring" in a husband, miss?' she'd asked, then piped down when she saw the icy look on my face.

I was not prepared for the stormy air at dinner. My father had been 'reliably informed' that I had been at the Palace of Westminster – 'eavesdropping', as he put it, on the debate. He was almost as furious with poor Mrs Willow as he was with me. To her credit, Mrs Willow never blamed me in these situations, but took all responsibility, which I could not allow.

'Papa, it was all my idea, I assure you. Do not blame Mrs Willow. I am interested in politics, and especially in the slave trade. It is too cruel. I can hardly bear to think of what is happening just a couple of miles from where we sit. I wish you involved me more in your work. I am curious,' I explained.

'Well, you shall contain your curiosity. You shall not come back to Westminster and you shall end this ridiculous preoccupation at once!' raged my papa. 'You are disgracing the family. Our forefathers worked hard so that we might enjoy certain privileges, and we must honour the Musgrove family name.'

'And might I ask, Papa, who told you of our presence in the Chamber?' I enquired with icy calm.

'It was a very kind and decent young man who is worried for your safety – Mr Hughes. And a finer young gentleman you could not hope to find,' my father snapped.

So Mr Hughes had been telling tales on me. I almost choked with anger. In a fit of indignation after dinner, I dashed off a note to Marcus, agreeing to go on the march with him. Then I settled down with Dinky to read my scribbled notes from the meeting I had attended.

Slaves are brought to Britain by sea, the ships often docking at the East India Docks . . . The African Lady pretends to be a spice and coffee cargo vessel but has a hidden hold for slaves in the lower decks. She is due at the East India Docks on June 17th.

All of a sudden I had an idea. I decided to write to Lucy as well.

8th June 1803
Musgrove House

Dear Lucy,
　　How are you? All well with Mr A? Are you going to the Devonshires' salon party on Thursday 17th June? If so, perhaps you and Lady

Lennox would care to stay here for the night after-
wards, as we are so much closer to the
Devonshires' townhouse? You see, I need your
help with a mission I am planning after dark. I will
tell all when I see you. Please let me know if you
can help.

Your loving friend,
Sophie
xxx

I received a letter of agreement from Lucy the very next day, and carefully planned a midnight outing to the docks. It would not be an easy task, but I wanted to know if all that I had heard about the terrible conditions in which the slaves were kept was true – and this was the only way to do it. But how would we get there, and what if we were recognized?

It became clear to me that a disguise would be essential. I immediately thought of borrowing some garments from Lily so that Lucy and I would look as if we were in service. I asked her if I could borrow two sets of clothes.

'What for, Miss Sophie?' she asked.

'I'm afraid I can't say. I'm sorry to be so vague, but trust me, Lily, it is for a good purpose.'

Lily looked concerned but agreed to bring me what I wanted, so with the clothes sorted out I turned my attention to transport. Sid had more or less agreed to take me out on another mission, but I felt guilty about it. If he were caught, I knew he would be sacked and might not get another job without a reference, but the thought of taking an anonymous hackney to the docklands was scary. I had heard tales of girls being attacked by the drivers. There was no way round it: I would have to approach Sid.

On the following Thursday evening I hid everything we would need in the bottom of my wardrobe and set off for the Devonshires' house with Mrs Willow. The evening was a bit of a bore, with a poetry reading and a musical recital. It might have been enjoyable in normal circumstances, but Lucy and I were bursting to get back. I was dying to carry out my plan and Lucy was itching to hear about it.

As soon as the evening's entertainment was over and Lucy and I were alone in my bedroom, I told her of my plan. I explained that I needed to be informed for the march I was taking part in – and so I wanted to sneak on board a slave ship at the docks!

'Sophia! That sounds incredibly dangerous!' Lucy

gasped. 'What if we are caught? We might be thrown in one of those horrid gaols I have heard of where people eat rats and drink rainwater!'

'Don't worry, Lucy. We will only have a look and we'll only go on board if no one is watching,' I promised.

'Well . . .' said Lucy thoughtfully. For a moment she looked bewildered, but then she smiled. 'Marches? Midnight missions? Mr Stevens? Are you sure this is the same Sophia Musgrove?' she asked.

'No, this is the *new* Sophia Musgrove!' I told her.

'I see,' she laughed. 'Well then, East India Docks, here we come!' and she started to change into Lily's dowdy working clothes.

Just as we had finished getting ourselves ready, we heard Mrs Willow and Lady Lennox saying goodnight in the hallway. Then the handle of my bedroom door began to turn and I realized that Mrs Willow was coming in to say goodnight to me as she sometimes did.

'Hide!' I whispered to Lucy, and she dived hurriedly under the bed as I jumped under my counterpane and pulled it up to my neck.

'Goodnight, Sophie, dear,' said Mrs Willow, coming over to sit on the edge of my bed. 'Wasn't that a pleasant evening? Much more the sort of thing that you should concentrate on. And I heard from another of the chaperones that Mr Hughes is quite taken with you, Sophie. He talks of you often, apparently!' She chatted on like this for several moments. She is always rather talkative after an evening out and usually I am happy to chat, but tonight was different . . .

'I'm awfully tired, Mrs Willow,' I said sleepily. 'Shall we talk about the salon after breakfast?'

'Yes, of course. Sleep well, dear,' she replied. 'Remember your prayers, especially for your mama.' I prayed for my mother several times a day, so she had no need to remind me.

When she was gone, Lucy wriggled out from under the bed and we sighed with relief.

'Sid will be waiting in the back courtyard by now,' I told her. 'He muffles the horses' hooves with felt covers so that the servants don't hear us leave, and he covers the family crest on the coach with black fabric too, in case anyone should recognize it!'

'I say, this is *really* naughty, isn't it, Sophie? Have you done this before?' Lucy asked.

'Just once,' I whispered as we made our way down the back stairs of the townhouse.

'You're playing with fire!' Lucy exclaimed quietly.

'I like it,' she added. Then we caught sight of ourselves in the servants' mirror by the back door and gasped at how plain we looked.

'Gosh, not so pretty in these frumpy clothes, are we?' Lucy hissed.

I shook my head. 'Poor Lily, having to wear them all the time,' I sighed. And then we slipped out of the house and into the waiting carriage.

It took more than twenty minutes to reach the docks, and as we drew up I saw that we were going to have to explain ourselves to the watchman on the gate.

'Can you wait for us here, please, Sid?' I asked as we jumped down from the carriage.

'All right, miss,' Sid replied reluctantly. 'But this is no place for ladies such as yourselves. There'll be all sorts of trouble behind those gates. Mind how you go, the two of you, and hurry back!'

'What shall we say?' asked Lucy as we saw the gateman looking at us.

'Let's say our brother is on board a ship and we have urgent news for him,' I suggested.

'Good idea! Leave it to me. I have a good Cockney accent,' said Lucy, walking briskly towards the gate. 'And I've been dying to use it!'

Lucy was brilliant, mimicking the accent of her

maid, Daisy, perfectly while I struggled not to laugh. Soon we were ushered through the huge wrought-iron gates.

'You should be on the stage, Lucy Pennington!' I observed.

'That would be the best fun. Can you imagine?' Lucy chirped. 'But Mr Archer would never approve. He's the respectable sort.'

I didn't respond to that since I had grave doubts about the respectability of Mr Archer. However, I had no proof and I was still determined not to worry Lucy on the basis of unfounded gossip.

Besides, there were other things to think about . . .

The first thing I noticed was the strong smell that filled the air – a mixture of engine oil, alcohol and salt water. Happily this noxious combination was somewhat masked by the sweeter scents of cinnamon, cloves and nutmeg coming from the spice ships. We picked our way through coils of rope, old pieces of timber and general debris that lay about the place.

There were people everywhere. Sometimes they seemed to be quarrelling, but then they would erupt into raucous laughter. Dockers, sailors and soldiers bustled to and fro, some on business, some clearly enjoying their shore leave a little too much as they lurched drunkenly along the dock.

There was filth and squalor everywhere we looked, but there was a merriment to the place too, with sailors singing sea shanties outside the taverns, and dockers working busily to load food or unload cargo from the ships.

We made our way towards a large ship that seemed to be in the process of berthing. Sailors were still high up in the rigging, adjusting the ropes and sails. I recognized the name on the side – the *African Lady* – and my heart pounded with excitement. I was immediately reminded of my mission – to see for myself the conditions of slaves on board the ships. Then, at last, I would know the truth of what I'd heard – and be able to look the other activists in the eye, and contribute meaningfully to their discussions.

'This is the one, Lucy,' I whispered. 'Let's slip on board when the crew disembarks. We can hide down here and wait,' I added, spotting some netting which would form a handy screen through which we could watch proceedings.

'I'm not going on board if we might be caught,' Lucy said firmly. 'I couldn't bear to be kept here. It reeks of sweat and sewage!'

'I know. Don't worry,' I reassured her. 'We won't

venture onto the ship until we're sure it's safe. I just hope the crew will leave soon. Then we will see with our own eyes how these slaves are being treated.'

Lucy bit her lip nervously. 'Oh, Sophie, what if we don't get off alive? Who will know that we have perished on the *African Lady*? I don't think we should go on board at all. Please don't go!' she begged.

'If you can't face it, just wait for me here,' I said. 'You have already proved yourself the most loyal of friends. But I must take this chance to see the truth for myself.'

However, Lucy shook her head at that. 'No! I will not let you go alone,' she said. 'If you go, I go!'

We watched and waited. And the waiting was awful. I was afraid I might lose my nerve if we couldn't make our move soon.

Once the ship was safely tied alongside the dock, a few sailors came ashore, followed eventually by a man who looked as if he could be the captain. Meanwhile, a crowd of people – men and women – gathered alongside the ship, ready to help carry the heavy crates to shore. I remembered that the *African Lady* supposedly carried only coffee and spices – the slaves were kept in a hidden hold.

As we watched the hustle and bustle from our

hiding place, it occurred to me that all the activity might provide our best opportunity to board the ship. Who would notice two more people amongst so many?

'Now's our chance,' I whispered to Lucy. 'We will simply mingle with the crowd. Nobody will notice us, especially dressed as we are.'

Lucy nodded and we seized the moment, emerging from our hiding place and slipping in amongst the throng. We kept our eyes down and made our way up the narrow gangplank.

As soon as we were on board, we were hit by a terrible stench, much worse than anything we'd smelled on the dock. It was mixed with coffee, cinnamon and nutmeg, but the odour of human waste was unmistakable. It was so awful that we had to put our handkerchiefs to our mouths as I tried to work out where to look for the hidden living quarters.

Making my way between boxes marked COFFEE and NUTMEG, I headed for a small staircase that descended into the ship. As I neared the top of the stairs, I saw a sailor coming our way, so I grabbed Lucy's hand and drew her down behind one of the crates.

'I feel seasick!' whispered Lucy.

'Lucy, the ship is in dock, not at sea,' I replied. But the fact was that the ship was bobbing about on the water, and that gave us some hint of the rough journey those on board must have suffered in storms and high seas.

As soon as the sailor had passed, we moved on again. I guessed that the captain would be eager to get the slaves off his ship as quickly as possible, since he could be fined if they were discovered. So I knew we had no time to lose.

The air below decks was thick with the scent of spices mixed with human sweat and ordure, which made normal breathing difficult. It was also very dark. Only a few lanterns hanging at intervals lit our way with a smoky, flickering light, and we dared not carry one with us for fear of drawing attention to ourselves. We kept following stairs downwards until we were in the bowels of the ship. There I could hear the low moans of people in pain and I felt sure we were nearing the hold where the slaves were kept.

Following the sound, we came upon a small wooden door. It was flush with the wooden wall in which it was set and was not immediately visible – especially in the dim lamplight. It was only those terrible cries that led us to it. Surrounded by the terrible smell and the moans of misery, I wanted nothing more than to flee the ship and go no further. But having come so far, I was determined that I would not flinch from my mission now.

Taking a deep breath, I pushed at the door and it swung open, revealing row upon row of people, chained where they sat. They were packed in tightly, with no space to stretch out, and had open wounds on their arms and legs from the shackles. One woman looked as though she had been whipped: we could clearly see the weals on her back, for the fabric of her dress had been ripped to shreds by the whip, and in one corner of the tiny room I saw handcuffs, thumbscrews and branding irons, which I recognized from the meeting.

The poor slaves gazed at us in fear and confusion, and for a moment I was so appalled by their plight that I thought I would be sick. Lucy was speechless with horror. Neither of us had ever seen such suffering. Our idea of discomfort is when the fire in our hearth goes out, or when we don't dance with the best catch at a ball. This was a level of human deprivation we had never imagined in our worst nightmares.

'We are not here to hurt you,' I said softly to some women and children who lay cowering in a corner. 'Indeed, we will try our best to help . . . .' I added feebly. I felt horribly ineffectual – what could I do alone? But as part of a group, and with Marcus by my side, I felt I really could help to bring about change. I was more determined than ever to take part in his work to stop the slave trade.

I saw that we could make no difference on board the ship, so when Lucy begged to get back onto terra firma, I agreed. Sid would be waiting and I had successfully carried out my mission – everything I had heard about the treatment of slaves appeared to be true.

As we quickly made our way off the ship and back towards the gates where we had left Sid, we saw beggars and drunks at every corner. The taverns had now closed and their customers had spilled out onto the docks, drunk and looking for a new source of entertainment. It was much more frightening than it had been on the way in.

Two men lurched towards us and one said, 'Give us a kiss, darlin'. Don't be shy!'

We did not respond, but to avoid the men we turned aside into an alley that ran behind a chandler's shop. It was a mistake, for as soon as we were past the shop, the two drunks stepped out in front of us from a side alley. They obviously knew the dockyards much better than we did and had seized the opportunity to cut us off.

I looked around wildly for help, but the alley was deserted and the docks were so noisy I knew no one would hear, much less come to our aid if we screamed. We were alone in a dark alley and the two men were advancing upon us.

Chapter Thirteen

'Give us your money!' said the shorter of the men, who reeked of alcohol.

'Or if you have none, then a kiss 'n' a cuddle instead!' cried his friend, who was taller.

They both laughed coarsely at that, and the tall man lunged towards Lucy and grabbed her round the waist.

'Mmm, pretty clean hair!' he exclaimed, sniffing at her blonde curls and pawing at the front of her dress with grubby hands.

I felt sick with fear, but at the same time I was furious – with the men, and with myself for bringing poor Lucy here in the first place.

'Lucy!' I cried as she was dragged away and the other man reached for me. I sidestepped away from his grasp; luckily he was so drunk that he stumbled to the ground when he tried to catch me. My attention was still fixed on Lucy, who looked as though she was about to faint. Her attacker was now pulling roughly at her clothing, and I ran forward to try and drag him away from her, but he was too strong for me and simply ignored my frantic attempts. Even though his accomplice was too drunk to be much of a threat, he staggered towards me again now, muttering oaths.

Our situation was now parlous. Lucy's clothes were ripped and she seemed too stunned to help herself. I *had* to save her. I looked desperately around the alley for inspiration and spotted a plank of wood lying against the wall of the shop. I grabbed it, and though it was too heavy for me to wield properly, I swung it at Lucy's attacker.

Whack! The man was felled. I turned and swung again. *Bonk!* The other went down too.

They were not seriously hurt – I think it was only the fact that they were drunk that caused them to fall so easily. As they started to struggle to their feet again, I ran to rescue Lucy. She had little strength left in her, but at least she was free of her attacker.

'Lucy! Come on!' I urged. 'We have to get back to Sid before they come after us. You can do it! We will be safe in a moment, dear!'

I looked around, still hoping for help from anyone

with any decency who might have seen our predicament, but the alley remained deserted. We couldn't go on as the men were in our way, so I grabbed Lucy's hand and ran with her back the way we had come. We stopped near the *African Lady* to rest behind the nets again and catch our breath. As we stood there, I saw Lucy's blue eyes fix upon the ship and open very wide. I followed her gaze. She was staring at the ship's gangway – and in particular at a man who stood there.

'Why, it's my Mr Archer!' she exclaimed in surprise.

'Oh!' I gasped. It looked as though the gossip that Lily had heard in Whistling Sparrows was true: Mr Archer really was involved with the slave ships. I did wonder momentarily if he might be of any help in our current predicament, but I fancied he would not relish being caught on board an illicit ship after midnight. And we should not have been there either. Still, I felt I must put Lucy's feelings first after all she had been through.

'Shall I go and fetch him, Lucy?' I asked.

'Oh, heavens, no! I am not pretty like this!' she replied immediately, and I couldn't help but smile – she was still concerned about her appearance in spite of all that had happened that night.

I was glad to leave him be, if for different reasons. He stood there on the gangway, chatting quietly to the ship's captain, who was heading back on board with a small barrel of ale. They obviously knew each other well and I thought I saw Mr Archer hand over a wad of banknotes, though it was hard to be sure in the dark.

As he turned to leave, we heard him call back to the captain, 'For God's sake keep them quiet below!' and after that I could be in no doubt that he knew all about the slaves.

'Let's give him time to leave the yard,' whispered Lucy. 'No wonder he is often caught up with his business affairs if he keeps late hours like this.'

I got the feeling that even in her fragile state, poor Lucy knew that Mr Archer could not be up to any good on the *African Lady*, but we did not discuss the matter; we had more pressing concerns. As soon as we were sure that he was safely gone, we joined hands and made a dash for the main gates. It was an immense relief to reach the other side and to see Sid jumping down from our carriage to help us inside.

'In the name of goodness, Miss Sophia! What have the pair of you been up to in there?' he asked, seeing Lucy's ripped clothes and anxious face.

I have never felt so ashamed. I felt awful for

bringing my dear friend to this place . . . And yet something within me had changed after the horrendous suffering I had witnessed – I knew it was important for me to have seen it with my own eyes.

'We were looking on a ship, Sid, to see how terrible it is for the slaves they bring over by sea. But then we were attacked. And Lady Lucy got the worst of it, to my deep regret,' I explained.

'Well, don't ever ask me to do this again. And this time, I mean it!' said Sid furiously, closing the door of the coach.

I tucked a blanket around Lucy to cover her ripped clothing.

'I wonder what my Mr Archer was doing there, Sophie,' she murmured.

'Try not to think of it tonight, dear,' I said, knowing how sad she would be when it dawned on her that Mr Archer was not the wonderful man she'd believed him to be. Not for the first time, I felt lucky to have met Marcus at the wedding. He was truly concerned about the slave trade. He was changing my life.

Back at Musgrove House, Lucy and I took off our shoes and crept upstairs as silently as we could. I was very relieved when Lucy was safely tucked up in bed in the guest room. We both slept in very late the next day, but luckily the Devonshires' salon was blamed for our exhaustion.

Lucy was very sweet about the whole dockyard incident, and I knew she would be discreet. But even though she was concerned about Mr Archer's dealings at the docks, her feelings towards him had not changed. Perhaps when she blocked out the horror of her attack she also conveniently erased her memory of Mr Archer talking to the captain of the *African Lady*.

I was appalled to think of the danger we had faced, but my mind was quite skewed by my new knowledge of slavery, and all I could think of was how important it was to go on the anti-slavery march.

Lucy and I hugged each other goodbye with extra feeling when she and Lady Lennox took their leave. Once they were gone, I lay on my chaise, reading a lovely letter from my mother – who sounded quite jolly, thank goodness.

There was a knock at my door. It was Hawkes with a note, and I immediately recognized Marcus's writing. As soon as he'd left I ripped open the envelope.

18th June 1803

My dear Miss Musgrove,

I hope this finds you well. Everyone at the meeting was most impressed that a young lady of your exceptional background should be willing to support our cause. Thank you for coming, dear heart!

I cannot think of anyone closer to my dreams of the perfect lady than you. I am no poet, but I wish I were in order to do justice to my feelings for you.

I have need to speak to you privately and most urgently. I know it is hard for you to escape from your chaperone, but could you meet me in Hyde Park, by the fountain, at midnight tomorrow? I know this is a very short distance from your house – I have your safety and well-being at the forefront of my mind. Please reply to the following address if this suits and I will check there for mail:

The Clock Tower Hotel
Clerkenwell
London

I trust you can help me – your spirit is so pure. We were fated to meet, I am sure of it.

Marcus Stevens
x

I was so excited. Why did Marcus want to see me again so quickly? It was very romantic – meeting by the fountain after dark! I couldn't wait to find out what he wanted of me. I replied immediately to promise that I would be there – and the die for our secret rendezvous was cast!

I could hardly eat dinner the following evening. Thank goodness for Dinky, who often sits at my feet under the table, retrieving scraps – a habit which has taken two inches from my hips and added two to his, poor dear! When Papa and Mrs Willow had retired for the night, I dressed myself warmly and waited until a quarter to midnight before creeping downstairs, slipping quietly out of the house and setting off for the park. I was incredibly excited, though a little nervous too after my experience at the docks.

It was a cool evening and I shivered as I sat on a bench by the fountain. My heart was beating at a great pace – at first with excitement, but as time wore on, with fear. There was no sign of Marcus and I began to imagine the two drunken thugs from the docks, lurking in the bushes, ready to attack me.

I stood up and began to pace about, not knowing which way to turn. The streetlamp above me flickered in the breeze, sending the shadows dancing around me. And then I heard a rustling in the bushes, and I was frozen to the spot with fear.

But just as I was thinking of running for home, Marcus appeared out of the shadows, looking amazingly handsome in his naval-style greatcoat. I was struck by the fact that he always wore light breeches and leather over-boots, with a smart white shirt and patterned waistcoat. I liked his choices well; he was not a dandy, but was very stylish nonetheless, and it did not escape me that his clothes looked so fine because they adorned a well-toned body. I assumed that he was so fit from his boxing.

'My dearest Miss Musgrove – Sophia! Do forgive my tardiness, please! You are the truest as well as the most beautiful of ladies. Thank you for coming.' He took my cold hands in his and pulled me towards him in the moonlight.

I longed for his kiss, but he merely brushed his lips across mine, saying, 'I must not. It is wrong of me before we are committed to each other.' Instead he held me close and I felt perfectly protected.

'What did you want to discuss with me, Mr Stevens? It seemed so urgent,' I said.

'I hardly like to trouble you with it,' he replied, going on to explain that with a period of activism for the anti-slavery cause looming, the group needed to produce some information booklets about the slave trade to hand out to Londoners.

'That's a good idea,' I said. 'People need to be educated about its horrors. Until recently I, for one, knew nothing of it.'

'But you see, Sophia, we need some very valuable information for these pamphlets – information to which you might have access!' he declared. His face was close to mine and I could see his eyes shining with passion. I'm sure it was for the cause, but I hoped a little of it might have been for me too.

'*I* have this information?' I responded, failing to follow his thinking, as I was rather distracted by his striking good looks and the wonderful smell of gentleman's soap and mint.

'Yes, my darling. This information will almost certainly be among your father's private papers – we can use some of that information to our advantage. We really believe it can help to bring an end to this cruel practice much more quickly,' he explained.

'Oh, I see,' I muttered, although all I really saw was his handsome face before me.

'You would play a key part in bringing an end to the slave trade,' he continued. 'Think of it, Sophia! The movement would be for ever in your debt! And such an achievement would bind us together for ever,' he said.

I shivered, partly with the cold, but also partly with the thrill of excitement that ran through me at his words. Ever thoughtful, he took off his overcoat and wrapped it around me, holding it in place protectively.

A million thoughts were running through my head. I was elated by Marcus's tenderness for me, but I was also surprised by his request. Perhaps I had thought that our meeting was to be of a romantic nature, but of course, a principled man like Marcus would never let romance get in the way of his fight against social ills. That was what I loved about him.

'Mr Stevens, what are these papers you speak of?' I asked.

He seemed pleased that I was considering his request. 'They are called: *The Cost of the Abolition of the Slave Trade*, and *Addington's View on Slavery*. They have been distributed among only six major politicians. Your papa is one of them,' he explained.

'How do you know of these documents?'

'There are those in the upper echelons of government who spill the beans to us after a pint or two of ale, Sophia,' he told me.

'I would like to help, Mr Stevens – Marcus, but I have much to consider,' I said. 'It is, after all, theft, isn't it?'

'The thing about growing up, Sophia, is understanding that though an act may seem wrong, if it achieves much good then it can be justified. But I quite see how hard this is for you,' he said. 'Of course, you must think it over, but I would be so proud of you. And just think what a great cause you would be furthering and how much needless suffering you would help to avert!'

'I will think about it very hard. I would like to help, of course,' I promised.

'I knew you would understand. You are quite the most wonderful young lady. Special – no, *unique*!' he said.

I smiled. 'I didn't do brave things until I met you,' I told him.

He took my hand and pressed it to his lips. 'I must not keep you out in the cold. Let me walk with you to the pavement. I would hate any harm to come to you. You mean so much to me,' he said, and we set off through the silent park.

Once outside the park, we stopped. Marcus kissed my hand again and looked at me lingeringly. And then, before I realized what was happening, he kissed me full on the lips. 'I cannot resist you!' he sighed. 'Goodnight, and sweet dreams, my love.'

'Goodnight, Mr Stevens,' I whispered, and ran back to Musgrove House. I stood in the portico and watched him disappear into the misty night. I had meant to tell him about my trip to the docks with Lucy, to prove how committed I was to the cause, but there hadn't been time.

Still, it had been the most amazing encounter. I felt dizzy from his unexpected kiss, and as I settled down in bed, I reflected that somehow, the closer I grew to Marcus the more I felt alone in my normal life. My mother was miles away from me, struggling with her health, and Mrs Willow chatted constantly about the new baby. My dear sister had gone to live with her new family, and my relationship with my father was becoming strained, to say the least. Marcus was my main friend now, along with Lucy. I didn't want to let him down, and yet it was a lot that he asked of me this time.

Chapter Fourteen

I had a restless night and was still very preoccupied with my thoughts when Lucy dropped by the following morning.

She was her usual bubbly self and looked stunning in a beautiful new gown of deepest cobalt blue, trimmed with heavy lace. 'Sophie, I must talk to you!' she said as we walked around the walled garden together while Lady Lennox and Mrs Willow took tea together in the morning room.

'What is the news?' I asked curiously.

'It's Mr Archer. I've had such an exciting letter from him. I *think* that he means to propose to me!'

'Oh, what makes you think so, Lucy?' I asked.

'He writes that "two loves intertwined are better than one"!' she explained. 'And he says that next time we meet, he will tell me his first name! Obviously he has marriage in mind, don't you think?'

I hesitated, trying to read Lucy's expression. I wasn't sure whether she had doubts about Mr Archer after seeing him at the docks, or whether she had entirely banished that memory. I could certainly see no sign that it was troubling her now. 'Yes, I do think so,' I agreed. 'But are you happy?' I asked cautiously.

'I think so,' she replied. 'He is away overseas on business for six weeks now, but he is writing to me almost every day. His letters are very sweet, and have been getting sweeter. Oh, I do love him so!' she cried.

I was fearful of spoiling Lucy's merry mood but felt I must take this opportunity to talk to her while Lady Lennox and Mrs Willow were still safely out of earshot. 'It would be very comforting to establish just what he was doing at the docks when we saw him, Luce,' I ventured.

'What? Oh, Sophie, don't give it another thought. He is a businessman. It was much more shocking that *we* were at the docks,' she responded cheerfully, but it was clear that she did not want me to pursue the matter further. Indeed, she changed the subject, turning to me with a concerned expression. 'Sophie, what's wrong with you, dear? You are very quiet and pale this morning. Please don't say you have been to the docks again alone?' she whispered, mindful of the gardeners' big ears. We didn't mind what Lily heard, but some of the other staff were not to be trusted.

'No, not the docks,' I replied.

'Then you *have* been somewhere!' she exclaimed. 'Where was it, Sophie?'

'I went to meet Mr Stevens in Hyde Park last night!' I confessed, expecting her to be mightily impressed.

'Sophie! Did he suggest such a thing? Has he no thought for your safety . . . for your reputation?' she demanded incredulously.

'He thinks of higher things, Lucy,' I tried to explain. 'He is full of concern for me, but he is different from other men.'

'He is different indeed! I'll say that much for him,' Lucy agreed, pursing her lips. 'But why did he want to meet you?' she asked.

'He has asked me to do a favour for him. To borrow some of my father's papers that relate to the slave trade,' I admitted.

'What? You call that a favour? I call it a *crime*. And what response have you given him?' she asked.

'I told him that I would think about it,' I replied quietly, somewhat wrong-footed by Lucy's horrified reaction.

'Sophie, your dear father – who would rather die than think of you alone in the docks, or the park, by night – would be destroyed if you did such a thing,' Lucy said firmly. 'Would you really betray him in favour of this Mr Stevens, of no fixed abode? I have asked all over London for information on his background, but he is slippery, I can tell you,' she informed me.

I was very tempted to say, *What about your Mr Archer? Have you not checked up on him?* but I knew that Lucy meant well: I did not wish to hurt her after all she had been through at the docks on my behalf.

'I expect I will refuse,' I said, and then changed the subject to news of Estella. Her latest letter, which had arrived that very morning, worried me greatly. 'Estella sounds nothing like herself in her letters, Lucy,' I told my friend. 'Listen to this:

> *"I fear I am not pretty any longer. Percy seems to detest me at times, but as you know, Sophie dear, my ways are very annoying, are they not? Remember how I used to annoy you?"*

Lucy was shocked. 'She sounds very low! How alarming!' she said. 'Estella could not be *less* annoying.'

'I know,' I agreed. 'I think Mr Dovetail is cruel to her. He is truly insufferable!'

'Oh, dear, we long to be married, but then it can be so disagreeable, can't it?' Lucy sighed. 'What a worry! Perhaps you should go and visit her.'

I nodded. I was so full of my own concerns that I could not bear the thought of leaving London just yet. But Lucy was right. My sister needed me. *I shall go after the march*, I decided. *I must.*

But at dinner that evening it transpired that Papa had already conceived a plan for me to visit my sister – and sooner than I had intended.

'Sophia, I will not lie to you,' he began. 'I am worried about your interest in political affairs. Such things should not concern you. You should be busying yourself with cross-stitch and the pianoforte, as Estella has always done – and yet I have heard that you intend to march through the city in support of the anti-slavery lobby! Such an event is no place for a young lady. You should be ashamed of yourself for even considering indulging in such unladylike behaviour. Can it be true that you planned to march with such radicals?' he asked.

'I have been asked to attend, it is true. But I cannot think who would give you this information,' I said, trying to remain calm, despite my anger at his insulting attitude.

'My source is confidential,' Papa replied cagily, as though he had promised someone that he would not blurt out their name, but I guessed at once that it must be Mr Hughes. He had already seen fit to tell tales on me once. In fact, all the squabbling with my father had begun after Mr Hughes had told him that I was at the debate in the Palace of Westminster. How I hated that interfering busybody! 'I am not ashamed of myself, Papa,' I continued. 'Far from it. Someone in this family has to do something to defend the rights of those suffering people that the government of this country treats with such disregard. I've seen you *talk* about helping these people, but nothing changes, and you could do so much *more*. I don't know how you can sleep at night. You always taught me to be *kind* to others. Indeed, *I* am ashamed of *you*!' I blurted out.

'Sophia! You know nothing of my work. You should trust me to do the right thing, just as your mother has always done. Leave men's work to the men, child,' he said furiously. Then he sighed. 'I know not what foolish notions have taken over your mind, but of one thing I am sure – you will leave as soon as possible for Dovetail Hall to visit our dear Stella. God knows, I am worried sick about her too. I fear I may have to insist that both she and her husband come to stay with us.'

Oh, dear Lord, Mr Dovetail in the household would finish me off, I thought, but of course I was just as worried about Estella as Papa. And as our family is rather more elevated than the Dovetails, I knew that he could insist on such an arrangement – which I would be more than happy to endure for dear Estella's sake.

I knew there was no point in fighting my father any further. 'How long will I be gone, Papa?' I asked.

'Three weeks,' he replied. Of course, he knew this meant I would miss the march.

I was devastated – I felt I would be letting Marcus down. He didn't even know that I had risked my life at the docks to learn more about the slave trade. He would think I was feeble and cowardly. There was much that I wanted to explain to him, but what could I do? I lived under my father's roof and had no choice but to do as he said. And besides, some inner voice was telling me that my sister needed me too.

Chapter Fifteen

*M*rs Willow, Lily and I made our way to Dovetail Hall in Oxfordshire one sunny morning a few days later. Sid drove us there, with Silverbell and Berry pulling us along. My beloved Cloud was resting in the mews as he was lame.

When we reached Dovetail Hall, which was mercifully closer to London than Whistling Sparrows, we were met by an almost unrecognizable Estella. She looked thin and her movements were twitchy and nervous.

'Come in, sister dear, and thank you for coming,' she said. When Mrs Willow hugged her, she held on for so long we thought she would never let go, and I saw that her eyes were red and swollen.

'Now, now, Estella. You will tell Willow everything that is troubling you when we're settled. Agreed?'

Mrs Willow always spoke of herself in the third person like that when she was trying to comfort us.

At that, a voice boomed down from the stairwell: 'There is nothing to tell, Mrs Willow. My wife becomes over-emotional. I'm sure it is a characteristic you know well,' said Mr Dovetail.

'Actually, no, Mr Dovetail. She seems very unlike herself to me,' retorted Mrs Willow tartly.

I was delighted to see that she was not cowed by Mr Dovetail. He was unbearable. I put my arm around Estella and she told us that other guests were expected for a house-party weekend, with salons, dinners and country walks.

'Oh, how jolly,' I said, trying my best to cheer her up. 'Who is coming?'

'Some of the people who attended our wedding,' she replied. 'The main one you will know is Mr Dovetail's old soldiering companion and Lord Sandford's cousin, Mr Hughes. He's so very dashing, isn't he, Sophie?'

My face froze. 'He's . . . supposed to be, yes,' I mumbled, wondering how on earth I was going to get through this ordeal. I recovered my cheerful expression as quickly as I could for my sister's benefit, but my first clear thought once I was settled in my room was to write to Marcus.

Dovetail Hall
Banbury
Oxfordshire

22nd June 1803

Dear Mr Stevens,

I have left London on an urgent family matter and regret that I will not be able to attend the march, even though I had prepared for it well by visiting the African Lady at East India Docks. You may be assured that it is only a matter beyond my control that prevents me joining the march. I am still considering the other matter regarding the documents and will come to a decision soon.

I look forward to our next meeting. I feel at my happiest when I am with you.

Yours sincerely,
Sophia Musgrove
xxx

Most of the guests arrived around midday and were served with a cold lunch. When afternoon tea was served at four o'clock, I sat on a plump brocade sofa in the day room, which is filled with chandeliers and candelabra and over-stuffed furniture. I sat next to a pleasant girl from Bath, called Susannah, and chatted about the Season for a while, but when she went to find her fiancé, the vacant spot on the sofa was filled by none other than Mr Hughes.

I was still sure that he had told my father about the march, just as he had blabbed about seeing me at the slavery debate. He was a telltale, that was for sure. If only I had not mentioned it to him that day at Harvey's. Me and my temper! But I could not ignore him in such circumstances, and to tell him what I really thought of him would have been rude to Estella as our host. I felt that she had enough problems of her own, so I was forced to make painful conversation with him.

'How are you, Miss Musgrove?' he enquired.

'Quite well, thank you, Mr Hughes,' I responded curtly. There was a look of confusion on his face at my response – no doubt he had no idea why I detested him so much, but I didn't care. I was furious and very worried about Marcus being disappointed in me.

'How is your mother progressing in her confinement?' he enquired.

'She is very tired,' I replied. 'We are looking forward to the delivery so that she may begin to recover her strength – and so that we may meet our new family member, of course.'

'Yes, it is very exciting for you all,' he agreed.

At that point we were interrupted by Mr Dovetail's cousin, Leonora Pink. She was wearing a pale lavender dress, in the new style, but it was very much fancier than those Lucy and I admired. It was covered with bows, pearls and ribbons, which she fiddled with incessantly. She is amazingly pretty, in a perfect, doll-like way, and yet there is a flatness to her presence somehow, as though she were a one-dimensional cut-out.

She sat extremely close to Mr Hughes. 'I have been meaning to talk with you since the wedding,' she told him. 'Do you remember you said that you would teach me to aim with a bow and arrow? Well, Cousin Percy is setting up just such a sport on the lawn now. Would you come and show me how it's done?' she simpered.

Ever the gentleman, Mr Hughes rose to escort her down to the lawn. *What a relief!* I thought. Leonora was doing me a huge favour by relieving me of the infuriating Mr Hughes.

'Do come and join us, Miss Musgrove,' she said over her shoulder. 'If you are lucky, Mr Hughes will show you how it's done as well.'

I didn't have much choice but to agree to join them presently, and to be honest, I thought it might be fun. My little brother, Harry, had taught me archery tricks during our long summers at the Daisy Park. I was sure I had a move or two up my sleeve to outshine the simpering Leonora Pink. And perhaps even Mr Hughes!

When I went up to change into a more comfortable dress for the purposes of triumphing with the long-bow, I complained to Lily about the detestable man.

'Excuse me for saying so, but I think he's a very fine gentleman,' said Lily.

'Lily, he is not, I can assure you. Do you know that he told my father about the slave trade march and has probably ruined my chances with Mr Stevens for ever? He meddles, Lily. I loathe him.'

'Maybe it wasn't him who told your father,' suggested Lily.

'Oh, it was him all right. No on else knew about it,' I insisted. When I was dressed in my plainest pale blue empire-cut gown with three-quarter-length sleeves, I brushed my wavy brown hair out loose.

'You look like a medieval warrior princess, miss!' exclaimed Lily. 'You are one of those lucky girls who needs no ornaments to shine.'

'Nonsense, Lily!' I said, but stole another quick look at myself anyway before leaving the bedroom.

'Can I come and watch?' she asked.

'Of course! You must hold my quiver of arrows!' I giggled. I marched down the stairs and out towards the garden as though heading for battle. Lily laughed as she followed on behind.

'Good God! Here comes Boadicea!' said Mr Dovetail, on seeing my arrival. Estella giggled and clung to his arm, but he shook her off irritably.

Meanwhile Leonora was insisting that Mr Hughes guide her arm through the process of firing.

'Ooh, it's so violent!' she trilled.

Mr Hughes swung round to greet me, leaving her to her own devices for a moment. Leonora immediately managed to drop the arrow, which skimmed past her foot, whereupon she wailed and cried out for a doctor. 'Really, Miss Musgrove. Can you not approach a gathering with a measure of decorum?' she complained as Mr Hughes helped her into a chair.

'I did not mean to unsettle you, Miss Pink. I am so sorry,' I said. As a few of the other guests fussed around her, examining her foot, which was completely unscathed, I made my way over to the archery field.

Leonora rapidly recovered her equilibrium when she saw me limbering up. 'I shall go first, if you please, Miss Musgrove!' she cried as she was helped back on to her dainty feet. 'Come, Mr Hughes,' she said. 'Help to guide me!'

Mr Hughes advised her on the position of her arms and hands and she released a very respectable shot.

There was a ripple of applause from the other guests. Leonora smiled a little smugly and motioned for me to step up to the mark.

I was suddenly determined to beat her. I could not bear to be outdone by such a silly, self-satisfied creature! Lily wished me luck and handed me an arrow. I tried to recall all Harry's tips about closing one eye and aiming for the centre. I took a deep breath and felt the eyes of the assembled throng upon me as I took aim – and fired.

Time seemed to stand still as I waited for the arrow to reach its destination. It wavered a little in the air and finally landed a long way off target. I was disappointed.

There was a collective murmur of 'Bad luck!' but Leonora was now warming to the competition. 'Ooh, shall we make a match of it, Miss Musgrove? I seem to be getting the hang of this!' she crowed.

'Very well,' I agreed with a smile, determined to do better on my next attempt.

With Mr Hughes's assistance, Leonora brought off another fine shot.

This time I concentrated harder and forced myself to block out all the distractions around me: the birds twittering, the chinking of china teacups and the low hum of conversation. Lily passed me an arrow and I took aim and released.

This one was much better! Almost as good as Leonora's in fact. A proper match was underway, only she was being coached by Mr Hughes and I was all alone.

She was a little ahead of me when it was time for the final shots, and the pressure was piled on us both.

Leonora stepped up and prepared herself for the all-important shot by loosening her arms and neck. She smiled over at me before raising her bow, and I could tell that she already thought victory was hers.

I could hardly bear to watch. The arrow flew through the air. It looked a little off, but it swung back in and made a respectable arrival at the target. Drat! I would have to do brilliantly to come out of this the victor.

Leonora wandered around proudly, accepting congratulations on her shot as though she had already won the contest. I took a moment to eye up the target carefully and remind myself of Harry's tips on controlling my elbows. Finally I released the arrow and watched with the assembled crowd as it flew straight into the bull's eye.

There was a huge cheer, especially from Lily.

'What a shot!' called Estella proudly. 'Well done, Sophie!'

I smiled over at Leonora and offered to shake her hand, but she looked away.

'I think I have sunstroke!' she complained, and went to sulk in the shade of a parasol.

'And now you, Mr Hughes,' I said, gesturing towards the target. 'It's your turn.'

He grinned, took off his jacket and rolled up his sleeves, determined not to be outdone by a girl.

With an intense look of concentration, he took aim and executed a perfect shot. Then another. And one more.

'It looks like we are a match for one another, Miss Musgrove,' he said. 'Perhaps *we* should have a competition?'

I grinned. 'Ah, but I would hate to embarrass you,' I told him, and with that I returned to the main house with Lily in tow. But I could feel Mr Hughes watching me all the way back across the lawn, perhaps with the flicker of a smile across his face. And I reflected that it was very hard to stay angry with such a likeable character.

Chapter Sixteen

My days at Dovetail Hall passed quietly after all the guests had departed. I hoped to receive a letter from Marcus, but day after day, nothing came. I worried that he was angry with me about missing the march, but I was finally rewarded with a delightful missive.

1st July 1803

My dear Miss Musgrove,
 I will miss you on the march. You are my inspiration now. What shall I do without you, sweetest? But do not fret. You are already doing so much good. I think of you often, or should I say always . . . I wonder what you are doing, and who you are with. I fret that you will become enamoured of another while you are gone. But I

*know you are loyal. Let me know when you are
back in the city.*

*Farewell until then,
Marcus Stevens x*

I was cheered immeasurably by this, and felt that
he really did care about me. But I could not help but
worry about Estella. She tried so hard to please Mr
Dovetail, and yet never met with his approval. He
seemed to find her conversation tedious, yet if she
was too quiet he called her a 'depressive'. She
couldn't do any right.

Estella was terribly low and in hopes of lifting her
spirits – and with her permission – I wrote to Lucy,
asking her to come and stay for a few days. To my
delight Lucy replied quickly to say that she was on
her way. Her bubbly personality always made Estella
smile and I prayed it would do the trick this time.

Meanwhile Estella, Mrs Willow and I fell into a
pattern of taking baskets of food to the poor in
Banbury each morning, and chatting in the salon
each afternoon while working on our cross-stitch. In
the evenings we were often joined for dinner by the
Dovetail parents and Leonora.

* * *

When Lucy and Lady Lennox arrived at Dovetail Hall, I was shocked to see that Lucy looked very weary; her eyes were red and sore with crying.

'Lucy, dearest, whatever is the matter?' I asked.

Lady Lennox shook her head. 'It is grave news,' she said. 'Grave news indeed!'

We huddled in the drawing room and Lucy revealed to us the nature of her distress. She held a handkerchief to her nose. 'It's . . . it's Mr Archer. He's in prison!' she declared through great gasping sobs.

'Prison!' I exclaimed. 'Whatever for?'

'He was bringing in slaves under illegal conditions on his spice ships,' she said. 'Remember we saw – I mean, heard about it?' she corrected herself, recalling that our chaperones knew nothing of our dockland visit.

Even though I had always had suspicions about Mr Archer, I was still shocked to hear that a close acquaintance of ours had actually gone to gaol.

Lucy was quite inconsolable for many minutes. 'I thought we would be married!' she sobbed. My heart bled for her. It was horrible to see my usually cheerful friend so distraught.

I gave her a hug. 'We must go to lots of parties and salons! We shall go to Brighton or Bath to catch the best summer parties if we must!' I told her firmly.

'We shall be the belles of every ball and that will take your mind off Mr Archer. Indeed, let's get those shoes you saw with the three-inch heels – and the dresses with the bust-enhancers too. People will say, *My, how they've grown! In every direction!*'

Mrs Willow and Lady Lennox giggled at this in a bid to raise Lucy's spirits. Those dear ladies love us as if we were their own daughters. Lucy rallied a little and we played cards together before lunch.

When I retired to my room later, I noticed a letter in my tray from my father.

The 3rd day of July, 1803
Musgrove House
Mayfair
London

My dear Sophia,

I do hope you have enjoyed your time with Estella and hope you bring good news of her health. Mama is making good progress, by all accounts, and she wrote to say that she was happy to think of you and your sister together. She asks what names you both like for the babe?

Sophie, I trust that your nonsensical rebellion

*will never happen again. And I'm sure it will
not if you lay aside your political notions and
allow me to continue with my work without
embarrassment. I know you will see sense and we
will continue as before. Indeed, I insist upon this.
Politics is not a suitable interest for a lady.
Hitherto I have indulged your wayward ideas, but
I am your father and in future you will do as I say.
A young lady needs to be guided and protected
and you must accept that I know best.*

*And do think of Sandford, my dear. I fear his
patience will not last for ever.*

*Safe journey and much love,
Papa xxx*

The nerve of him! I was furious at his determination to dismiss my political interests and ideas and
marry me off as soon as possible. It seemed he was set
on ruining my new life. Well, I would not allow it.
Now that I'd seen how miserable Estella was in her
wedded state, I felt no desire to rush into it myself.
Marriage seemed like one day of delicious partying
followed by an eternity of misery – and Papa would
have me packed off to Mellorbay Hall as Lord
Sandford's new wife in a flash!

And so I resolved to take my father's papers for Marcus. Surely he would be pleased and impressed with me then. Papa's approval was no longer necessary to me.

It was hard to say farewell to Lucy when she left a few days later, but even more difficult to part with my sister when my own stay came to an end. I really hoped that she would find the courage to stand up to Mr Dovetail, but it did not seem likely. Mrs Willow fretted on the journey back to London. 'She's not herself, dear girl!' she said at least a dozen times. Lily and I entirely agreed, but we were all powerless to help.

Chapter Seventeen

I was delighted to see Harry sliding down the stairs in a pillowslip when we got back to Musgrove House.

'Sophie! Hello!' he cried. 'Just the person. Can you come out into the garden and play Knights with me? You can be the damsel in distress!'

'All right, Harry,' I agreed, laughing. 'I'll be out in a moment.'

I ran up to my room and quickly wrote to Marcus to tell him that I was about to go in search of the papers he wanted. He replied immediately by special messenger.

Thank you, Sophia, darling. You are a true heart in putting the cause before all else. Please let me know when you have the papers. I am so proud of you! Indeed, my feelings for you grow and grow.

I have never felt this way before but you are different. You have the powers of an enchantress.

All my love,
Marcus x

I was honoured to be part of the select group that Marcus so admired. I really hoped that the papers would be in my father's office at Musgrove House and resolved to search for them as soon as I could.

That evening I sneaked into Papa's study. I rummaged and raked through everything, but could see no documents like the ones Marcus had described. Just as I was thumbing through a great pile of papers, I heard footsteps approaching.

'Oh no!' I said to myself. 'Papa will kill me!'

'What are you doing in there, Sophie?' asked a voice. I gave a sigh of relief! It was only Harry. 'Will you play at marbles, sis? I'm really bored.'

'Very well, Harry. I'll be with you in a minute,' I said.

He looked as if he was going to comment on my suspicious behaviour, but thankfully he was distracted by Dinky, and off he went to play with my dog until I was ready for marbles.

The following day Lucy and I met up in the Maison du Chocolat, along with Mrs Willow and Lady Lennox, of course. We waited until our chaperones were chatting, and then we began to talk properly.

'Lucy, how are you after your most terrible shock about Mr Archer?' I asked.

'Quite wobbly still,' she replied quietly. 'But if I am honest, I must say that I suspected it for a while. As you know, I hear all the gossip about everyone in London, and people were very cagey with regard to Mr Archer. And then, when we saw him at the docks . . . You did *try* to tell me, Sophie, but I'm afraid I didn't want to hear. And, you know, I think he *did* care for me, in his way,' she finished in a voice that told me that a part of Lucy had changed for ever.

'Lucy, you will fall in love again, and hopefully it will be with the right one next time,' I said.

She nodded. 'And how is your Mr Stevens?' she asked.

'He's wonderful!' I told her. 'In fact, Lucy, this pains me, but I would like to ask another favour of you with regard to Mr Stevens. The last one, I promise!'

'Oh, Sophie. You saved my life at the docks, but I could not go back there. I have nightmares about it still,' she cried.

'No, Lucy! I would not ask that of you. It is the matter of my father's papers,' I explained. 'I need your help in getting hold of them.'

Lucy frowned, looking thoughtful. 'Very well, I will help you,' she said at last. 'But first I must say this: if your Mr Stevens were a gentleman, he would not allow you to undertake such dangerous missions on his behalf!'

I ignored her caustic comment. I had no wish to argue with my best friend.

'Where do you suppose such documents will be filed?' she asked.

'Well, I've had a quick look in Papa's study at Musgrove House, but they are not there. I fear I will have to get into his private room the Palace of Westminster,' I revealed.

Lucy looked aghast. 'Oh, Sophie. What if we are found out? My dear parents would disown me!' she whispered.

'We will be careful,' I assured her. 'We will go over there one day when we know Papa is debating in the Chamber. We can easily search his office then, as long as we can slip past the guards,' I explained.

'Oh, all right then. So long as I don't have to steal anything, I'm game!' said Lucy.

I squeezed her hand. She was proving to be the

very best of friends to me, and all at a time when her own heart was broken.

I saw from my father's diary that he was involved in a debate on poor-house conditions on the following Monday, and I finally persuaded a reluctant Mrs Willow to take Lucy and me there to listen.

I felt treacherous as I placed his spare set of keys in my reticule before leaving Musgrove House that morning, but I was convinced that I was doing the right thing.

'Mrs Willow will fall asleep in the gallery, I am quite sure of it,' I whispered to Lucy as we walked towards Westminster, once our carriage had dropped us off on the Embankment of the River Thames. Mrs Willow was puffing along several paces behind.

'But what if she doesn't?' asked Lucy.

'Well, then I'll think of something else!' I replied anxiously. 'Anyway, once she is asleep we shall have to run to the private office wing. Lucy, if we should need to distract any gentlemen on the way, then you are the perfect person to do it!'

Lucy laughed and was about to protest, but we saw that we had reached the Palace of Westminster.

We took our seats in the public gallery. Dear Mrs Willow became quite sleepy, even before the debate began. It was a soporific atmosphere and she prefers people and gossip to politics. Once she was snoring softly, we slipped out of our seats and made our way across the vast building. Happily, it was deserted, as most people were in the Chamber.

We sped down corridor after corridor, each dimly lit by oil lamps. As luck would have it, we were unchallenged by any guards, and eventually we came to a passageway I vaguely recognized from a visit years before. We held our breath as we crept along, studying the nameplates on the doors. Finally I found the one with my father's name in gold letters upon it: THE RT. HON. LORD MUSGROVE, SENIOR MEMBER OF THE HOUSE.

We heard footsteps approaching. 'Someone's coming!' hissed Lucy, and we darted round a corner and then peeped out into the corridor.

We saw a guard in a red tunic stride past the end of the passageway. Once he was gone, we headed back towards Papa's office.

'Right,' I said. 'I'll go in while you wait outside and keep watch, Lucy.'

'Yes, all right. But do be quick, Sophie. I feel quite faint with nerves,' she said.

My heart was pounding as I tried key after key. I could hear the guard coughing at the end of the corridor and felt sure he was going to catch us at the door and take us to the Tower. But at last the door swung open and I slipped inside.

I looked about the office and was amazed to see portraits of myself, Mama and my siblings all around the room. On the desk there was even a calendar marked with our movements and birthdays. I didn't remember these things from my only previous visit so many years ago. There was a framed sketch I had made of a butterfly one summer at the Daisy Park, and a lopsided little wooden horse that Harry had carved. I realized then that Papa loved us all – but I could not afford to give in to nostalgia and sentimentality and fail in my task. I had a job to do for the cause.

I quickly found the key to the desk drawer. Inside there were piles of papers which all looked the same to me. I flicked through one pile after another, despairing of ever finding the right documents, until I found something that mentioned slavery.

I spread the papers out on the desk and hurriedly studied them. They were the ones Marcus wanted, I was sure. I was partly relieved and partly disappointed – perhaps deep down I was hoping to be able to tell him that the papers weren't there. But there was no time to agonize over my decision.

I grabbed the documents and ran to the door.

But just as I reached it, Lucy dived into the room and closed the door behind her.

'The guard's coming back this way!' she whispered.

Chapter Eighteen

We crouched down behind my father's desk. I could hear the footsteps now. They were coming closer. I had heard that the guards were all armed with swords and daggers. What if this one thought we were criminals and stabbed us to death?

The footsteps stopped and whoever it was opened the door. Lucy and I exchanged panicked looks. We were surely discovered!

There was silence. Presumably the guard was looking around. 'Lord Musgrove must have forgotten to lock his office,' he murmured.

I held my breath, praying he wouldn't decide to search for intruders, and after what seemed like an eternity, the door closed again. But I could not be sure if the guard was inside or outside the room. After crouching there for several uncomfortable moments, I plucked up the courage to peep out.

Slowly, slowly, I raised my head over the top of the desk. There was nobody there. We were alone. 'Come on, Lucy,' I said. 'Let's get out of here.'

'I fear we will be caught on our departure,' Lucy whispered anxiously. 'And the papers will be found on you, and we will be imprisoned! Sophie, we will be sent to the Tower of London!' she squealed.

I was not keen to encounter the guard either. 'Perhaps we could leave by the window,' I suggested, checking to see if this was indeed possible. We were a couple of floors up, but there was a sturdy tree near the building and I thought we might climb down that way. Lucy came over and peered out too, but she looked horrified when she saw the drop.

'No! I couldn't bear it!' she cried. 'I feel dizzy just at the thought. We will have to leave as we arrived. Let me look out into the corridor.' She hurried over to the door, opened it a crack and peered out. Then she beckoned to me. 'All clear!' she said.

I tucked the papers inside my undergarments and we ran as fast as our legs would carry us back towards the chamber. As we fled, we heard a guard shout: 'Who goes there? Friend or foe?' but we did not reply, and within minutes we were sitting next to Mrs Willow once again.

Despite a nagging feeling of guilt at having betrayed my papa, I was delighted to have accomplished my mission. I hoped Marcus would be pleased with me.

I had received a letter from him with instructions to take the papers to an anti-slavery meeting in Clerkenwell two days later. I couldn't wait to get rid of them. I was starting to feel a little guilty and was quite exhausted by the anxiety of having them in the house, so that night I sneaked out by the back door and took a hackney cab to the meeting.

When I arrived, I found Marcus at the door of the salon talking to a rather beautiful woman. He had that earnest look in his eyes that I had noticed whenever he talked about the slave trade. When he saw me, he bowed to the lady and excused himself to come and greet me.

'So was it a successful operation, Sophia?' he asked.

'Yes, very. Here are the documents!' I said, pressing them into his hands.

'Well done!' he said, evidently delighted by the success of my mission, then put the papers away in his case. He took my hands in his and squeezed them. For a short moment, as I gazed into his dancing blue eyes, it seemed that I had done the right thing and all the guilt and worry left me. But as soon as we entered the meeting, my doubts and fears returned. Firstly, I was surprised that he did not share the news of the arrival of the papers with the other members.

And then, as the meeting progressed, I felt more and more uncomfortable as the campaigners discussed the 'evil' character of gentlemen in government, such as my father. I thought of the family items I had seen in his office – I could not see him as evil at all.

'Lord Musgrove is a coward like the others,' said one campaigner. 'It is good that you see through him, Miss Musgrove! Blood isn't always thicker than water.'

This comment infuriated me, though I said nothing. They did not know my father to talk about him in such terms. But when I looked to Marcus for support, he seemed preoccupied.

Before long I was desperately wanting to leave. Added to which, I was worried that Mrs Willow might look for me in my room and find me gone. I said goodbye to Marcus, excused myself from the meeting and jumped into the hackney carriage that awaited me.

* * *

The next day Papa took Mrs Willow, Harry and me on a picnic in Hyde Park. It seemed to me that he was trying to spend more time with us these days, partly because Harry was missing Mama's tender touch, and partly, I think, because he was worried about my behaviour.

We played cricket and tried to catch butterflies by the Serpentine. Being with Papa in that relaxed setting reminded me of all the happy times we had spent together.

I watched a little ladybird scurrying over a leaf and remembered how he had always told us to treat wild things kindly and never to crush any of God's beasts, no matter how tiny. He was such a kind man, really, I thought.

I remembered the piggy-back rides he had given me at the Daisy Park when I was small, and the long winter evenings when he had taught me to write and play board games. There was the time when a local boy from Whistling Sparrows was threatening me with a stick and Papa came to my rescue like a roaring lion.

Amidst all these memories, I found myself regretting what I had done in my desperate attempt to help those who opposed the slave trade. But it was too late to undo my actions, and I tried to put the thought out of my mind.

A few days passed with no news of the papers or distribution of pamphlets, and I began to hope that nothing would come of my theft. However, I felt compelled to write and tell Marcus how monstrously guilty I felt about taking my father's papers: I told him that I would never do such a thing again. Marcus did not reply, which was unlike him.

I desperately needed to occupy my mind and distract myself from my guilty feelings, so I went to visit Lucy. We went through our vast selection of party invitations and other social engagements, mostly from out-of-town locations, keen to fill our diaries with outings.

'What we need, Sophie, is to buy some pretty new dresses, some new reticules, shoes and fans, then launch ourselves at every party worth going to!' she observed.

'Oh, Lucy, look at this letter,' I said, flicking through the pile. 'It's from Mr Hughes, asking if I might drop by his London home some time this summer. As if I would ever set foot in that man's house! The cheek of him. Does he want to squeeze some other secret out of me so that he can pass it on to Papa?' I said.

'Sophie, you don't know it was him,' Lucy pointed out. 'And anyway, have you heard from Mr Stevens lately? *He's* not been at *any* respectable parties this season.'

'Lucy, he doesn't go to mindless social dos. He is a thinker. It sets him apart,' I said defensively, though her comments did strike a chord with me. I was starting to wonder why Marcus had kept in regular touch with me before I got the papers for him, but not since.

'Or maybe he isn't welcome at polite functions . . .' said Lucy cryptically.

I had no interest in idle gossip, so I ignored this.

Lucy and I went on a shopping spree and bought lots of pretty new things to cheer ourselves up. The exercise wasn't entirely successful. My father never complained about all the items I put on his accounts and I felt a little guilty about spending his money when I had betrayed his trust and taken his private papers. But I was determined to throw myself into the party-going. I knew Papa would approve of that and I needed to take my mind off my recent mistakes. Also, I suppose I was trying to push away my anxiety about Marcus: he had not contacted me for days. I felt that I should never feel properly happy again.

One evening, as Lily was putting my hair up for a party in Grosvenor Square, with a satin band placed above my hairline in the new style, she asked me who was going to the party.

'Well, Lucy of course. And her sister, Catherine, I think,' I began. 'And as for gentlemen, most of the handsome ones, I believe. But I hope that Mr Hughes is nowhere in sight, or I might just throttle him,' I said.

'Excuse me, miss, for interfering, but why do you hate him so? He's a very fine man, it seems to me,' said Lily.

'Lily! You do not know him. He has betrayed me! He told Papa about the debate that I attended, and about the march I wanted to go on – which caused me to miss it,' I explained.

'But, Miss Sophie, there might be another explanation for how your father came to know about the march . . .' said Lily slowly.

'Such as?' I asked. 'I can't think of any!'

'You see, I'm sorry to say . . . I – I think I should tell you something,' Lily stammered.

'Lily what are you talking about?' I asked, turning around to face her. 'I don't understand.'

She looked down at her hands. 'I'm afraid it was me what told your father of that march thing. I was worried about your safety, miss . . .' she said.

I didn't respond. My heart was racing and I felt a mixture of confusion and anger.

Lily carried on. 'You see, Sid told me that you and Miss Lucy nearly died at the docks, and I heard you talking about the march, and I thought—' She stopped as I rose from my stool.

'Lily! How dare you meddle so! And how *could* you betray me to Papa? You had no right to listen to my private conversations and then pass information on to him. Are you his spy now?' I cried, shocked and distraught that Lily, whom I had always trusted, could betray me in this way.

'I'm sorry, Miss Sophie. Truly I am. It was only out of love and respect for you. I only did what I thought right,' she sobbed.

'Just leave,' I said quietly, trying not to cry. 'I will not have you working as my personal maid if I cannot trust you. You are dismissed! Pack your bags and be gone by morning,' I told her.

Lily bit back a sob and struggled to regain her composure. 'I'll go, but think on this, Miss Sophie. Mr Hughes is more true than that rogue Mr Stevens will ever be. He's trouble, that one, and no mistake. Even left Mr Hughes's poor sister for dead, so they say!' she blurted out. 'And if you don't trust me, you certainly can't trust him!'

And, with that, Lily ran from my room, sobbing and banging the door behind her.

Chapter Nineteen

Over the next few days I thought a lot about what Lily had said. Now I had something new to feel guilty for – wrongly accusing Mr Hughes of telling my father about the march. It seemed that every judgement I had made recently had been wrong. I no longer felt able to trust myself, and with Mama still away, Papa and I at loggerheads, poor Estella miserable in the country, and Lily now gone, I had never felt more alone. I thanked heaven for darling Harry and the long-suffering Mrs Willow.

'What did you and Lily quarrel about?' Mrs Willow asked me after Lily had left.

'It was something silly, but she had started to meddle, actually,' I replied.

Mrs Willow pursed her lips. 'If you go on confusing meddling with caring, you will be a very lonely girl,' she said sharply.

I started to keep a diary to unravel my feelings, writing:

Is it acceptable to betray another if the motive is pure? I have betrayed my father, but it was in the name of social justice. And if Marcus has betrayed me in the name of social justice, does that make his behaviour acceptable?

I cried myself to sleep with Dinky in my arms. I felt I did not deserve to be loved. Life was awful without Lily. For a start, Annie, my new personal maid, who had been promoted from general maid, was terrible at hair-dos; but more importantly I missed Lily's steady guidance and friendship.

Just as I was beginning to think that Marcus had completely abandoned me and I would never be happy again, an exciting invitation arrived by messenger. It was from him, and it invited Lucy and me to an after-show party at the King's Theatre. The production was *Romeo and Juliet* – very romantic.

I wrote to Lucy immediately:

Is it me being silly, or is it significant that he has

chosen such a romantic production to invite me to?

Lucy wrote back:

I would love to come with you. News has reached me that Mr Archer is to be kept in gaol for five years for his involvement in the illegal smuggling of slaves! I can't bear to think of him in prison for so long, though I know he doesn't deserve any sympathy. I must try to forget him. And a theatre party will be just the thing. I have never been to one before. La-di-dah! What shall I wear? Coachman! Take me to Mayfair, I have a dress to buy!

I giggled. Lucy was sounding more like her old self, thank goodness. We twittered back and forth by letter regarding hair-dos and shoes and 'looks' for the party. We also hatched a plan for slipping away from our chaperones . . .

Occasionally a society hostess who presents debutantes to the Royal Court will oversee an outing and give the other chaperones an evening off. On this occasion we pretended that this was what was happening, and simultaneously arranged a lovely treat for Mrs Willow and Lady Lennox – an evening at the opera, which we knew they could never resist. It was a great risk, but one we were determined to take.

I was very torn over my appearance. I knew that Marcus liked intellectual girls, but I did not want to look drab and dowdy at such an exciting evening party.

I set about piecing together an ensemble with a plain white gown, a white rosebud necklace and no rouge at all.

Lucy looked quite unbelievably beautiful when she appeared that evening. I did not feel jealous as such – I am always very proud of her. But she is far more womanly than I, and wore a very low-cut empire dress in soft lilac satin. (All right, I am a *little* jealous of Lucy!) Her hair was pretty too, woven with fresh flowers.

'Oh, I do miss my Lily!' I said, patting my slightly lopsided hair-do as we hurried to the theatre, which wasn't far from Musgrove House. We had seen Mrs Willow and Lady Lennox off earlier, assuring them that we would be collected by our chaperone; now we were free and ready to enjoy ourselves. Both of us were troubled by thoughts that we were eager to put out of our minds.

* * *

Lucy and I enjoyed the play enormously, although I was craning my neck the whole time to see if Marcus was in the audience. The actress playing Juliet was Diana Compton. She was beautiful, with a long, elegant neck and a sweet expression. I felt sure I had seen her before, but I couldn't think where.

On our way down to the foyer to meet Marcus afterwards, we heard a familiar voice behind us.

'Good evening, ladies. Did you enjoy the performance?' enquired Mr Hughes.

'Good evening, Mr Hughes. Yes, it was very fine,' I replied, blushing a little when I remembered how coldly I had treated him at our last meeting – and how unfairly!

'And now we are going to the after-show party,' put in Lucy excitedly.

Mr Hughes looked rather shocked at that. 'Be careful,' he warned. 'They are a wanton set. I myself am heading to Almack's for supper. Would you not care to join me there?'

'Thank you, no. We must keep our engagement,' I said. Lucy and I were far too intrigued by a theatre party to swap it for a simple supper.

'As you wish,' he replied with a slight bow. 'It was

a pleasure to see you both.' And he took his leave somewhat reluctantly.

'A wanton set,' breathed Lucy. 'I can't wait!'

We hovered awkwardly in the foyer until a steward asked, 'Are you for the party, ladies?'

'Yes, that's right!' said Lucy boldly.

'Then come this way, please,' he said.

We followed him through a maze of corridors and swing doors, all painted crimson with gold beading and lettering. Eventually we heard chatting and laughter and walked in on a scene of full-blown revelry.

The room was a riot of red and gold, with velvet walls and ornate pillars. It was very warm and the air was filled with the smell of wine and perfume. A hundred people or more laughed and danced and chatted merrily, giggling at risqué jokes and sipping delicious-looking drinks.

'Oh, my goodness,' I said to Lucy. 'This looks absolutely—'

'Wonderful!' Lucy interrupted.

I had been going to say 'wild' myself, but I decided that 'wonderful' would do just as well and let it stand.

It took a while to find Marcus – he was quite unsteady with alcohol, although he did look wonderfully handsome in an expensive, beautifully cut suit.

'Sophia!' he exclaimed. 'Come and meet the Prince of Wales!'

'We have already met,' I said, as politely as I could, given my opinion of him.

'Indeed we have,' said the Prince. 'And how nice it is to see you out in theatre-land, young Musgrove!' he added, running his gaze over me from head to foot. 'A bit thin, but plenty of promise. Good young flesh, eh?' he said to Marcus, as though I were a cow at market.

To my surprise, Marcus merely laughed. How odd, I thought, that so serious a person could behave with such abandon. He probably needs the relaxation, I concluded.

As the Prince of Wales tried to embrace me, despite the great distance created between us by his belly, I looked around, hoping for Lucy to rescue me. What I saw was Lucy reclining on a chaise longue, being fed grapes by the actor who had played Romeo.

I dared not interrupt her, as she was clearly having fun, so I endured the embrace, and then Marcus led me through the crowd, introducing me to his acquaintances. Most were quite incoherent with alcohol. *Perhaps I should have some wine,* I thought, suddenly feeling very straight and dull.

Marcus brought me a huge glass of red wine, which I drank too quickly, only to find him producing a decanter and refilling my glass. I covered the glass with my hand when he started to fill it the next time, but he insisted on topping it up 'in case' I wanted more.

I suppose I should have been flattered that so many men sidled up to me with compliments on my beauty, but for one thing I did not believe they were sincere, and for another, I was mightily hurt that Marcus showed no sign of jealousy at their advances. And I noticed that he was a little distracted by the leading lady from the play, the beautiful Diana Compton. I saw him stroke her hair affectionately, and at one point they were wound around one another in an embrace. Perhaps this is just the way theatre people behave, I thought. As I caught sight of the actress giggling, I suddenly realized where I had seen her before – she had been at the anti-slavery meeting in Clerkenwell when Marcus had seemed so preoccupied!

Watching the two of them together now, I suddenly realized what a fool I had been. Marcus loved another girl. And I had betrayed my very soul and my dear papa to please him. My thoughts overwhelmed me and the room started to spin. Vile, gargoyle-type faces seemed to leer at me as I negotiated the packed room in search of a chair.

I took a seat and put down my half-full wine glass, realizing that I was really rather intoxicated. By now, lots of people were kissing, or lying in drunken stupors. The mood of the party had changed from slightly naughty to completely dissolute. It all seemed horribly sordid.

Tears were close but I forced them back and stood up again, determined to go and look for Lucy. As I wove my way through the room, I overheard an exchange between two young men.

'How does that blackguard Stevens do it, eh? Where has he got his latest tranche of money from this time?' said a young dandy to his crony.

'From what I hear,' replied the other, 'he has made a packet selling some secret government papers. *And* he gets all the pretty girls, the cad! I hate him!'

Both men laughed. 'Yes, we hate him, but if he's offering lessons, I'll be at the front of the queue!' replied the first.

I gasped and had to lean against a pillar, feeling violently ill. I could barely take in what I had heard, and yet I knew at once that it was true. Marcus had asked me to betray my own father – not to help ill-treated slaves at all, but to line his own greasy pockets! How stupid I had been. I was racked with remorse, guilt and self-loathing. I had to find Lucy and get away from this den of sin. I felt as if it were contaminating every pore of me.

Eventually I found my friend behind a silk screen. She was very drunk and being fondled by a drunken 'Romeo'.

'Lucy, come with me, quickly!' I urged. 'I have to talk to you!'

'Sophie, please help me up. My head is spinning!' she said.

I offered Lucy my hand and pulled her to her feet. She stumbled towards me, and together we found the way out, which was not easy to do in the dim light. Gratefully we followed the flow of fresh air out onto the street.

I breathed a sigh of relief, but soon tensed again as I realized that we had been followed by a drunken lord. He was offensive and lecherous.

'Leave us alone. We have left the party!' I said.

'Oh, feisty? Just how I like them!' he said, grabbing my arm and pulling me to him.

'Help!' I cried as he drew me into an alleyway and forced me back against the wall. This time I was not free to look for a weapon and I feared that I would not be able to escape as Lucy and I had done at the docks.

I struggled, but my attacker kissed me hard on the lips and I heard Lucy crying, 'Sophie! Poor Sophie!' in a slurred voice. I knew that she was in no fit state to help me, and I had no idea how I was going to get out of trouble this time.

Chapter Twenty

Lucy had fallen quiet – I hoped she was all right, even though I had my work cut out fighting off my 'admirer'. But just as my strength was at an end, as if in a dream, a familiar face emerged above me. It was Mr Hughes. Lucy had gathered her wits and run to fetch him from Almack's.

'Mr Hughes!' I cried.

He took one look at the scene and pulled the amorous, drunken lord away from me. I buried my face in my hands and Lucy came to comfort me, while Mr Hughes punched my attacker and gave him a bloody nose, then pushed him back inside the doors of the theatre.

Mr Hughes came over to attend to me after that. He took off his cloak and wrapped it around me. Seeing that I was in no state to speak, he turned to address Lucy. 'Lady Lucy, what have you both been drinking?' he asked.

'A mixture of punch and wines,' Lucy revealed.

'Miss Musgrove may need a doctor. Where are your chaperones?' he asked.

'At the opera!' hiccupped Lucy, who was gradually sobering up.

'We cannot summon a doctor to Musgrove House at this hour,' I mumbled. 'That would waken the whole household! And I am not injured. I don't need a doctor.'

'I have a friend who practises medicine. He lives close by. If you agree to see him at his rooms, then I promise I will not reveal what has happened,' bargained Mr Hughes. 'But we must be sure that you are unhurt.'

'Thank you!' I said. 'That is very kind.'

Mr Hughes hailed a hackney carriage for us, and we arrived at the Warwick Street practice of his friend, Dr Maurice Wimpole.

It was very embarrassing to arrive like this, at such a late hour, but the butler went to fetch the doctor, and the lovely old man rose from his bed and trudged down to see us in his red dressing gown.

He checked me over in his surgery.

'She should be made to drink a pint of water and

sleep for a day, then she will be as good as new,' he told Mr Hughes.

Another hackney carriage was summoned, which took the three of us back the short distance to Mayfair.

'Enjoy the party, ladies?' Mr Hughes asked us.

'Not much,' I replied.

He smiled at me.

I tried to express my gratitude to him. 'Thank you,' I said simply. I had treated him very badly. Now I realized I had treated Lily very badly too. After all, she had only been trying to help, but I had been so blinded by my feelings for Marcus that I had not seen the dangers. Perhaps all my friends had cared about me more than I deserved.

Once we were safely delivered to Musgrove House, Mr Hughes bade us goodnight. He insisted that I drink a pint of water straight away and Lucy promised to oversee this. He seemed sorry to leave us, but eventually took his leave, promising to keep our secret.

After we'd both drunk a good deal of water, Lucy and I headed up to bed, clutching a lit candle each.

I looked from my window down onto the street below, where I spotted Mr Hughes. He turned round and saw the candlelight at my window. He waved up, as though saluting me, which made me smile. I saluted him back.

When I woke the next day, I lay in bed thinking over the evening's events. I was stunned by how Marcus had treated me at the party, and unbelievably grateful to Mr Hughes for rescuing me in spite of my recent coldness to him. The news that Marcus had sold my father's papers for money haunted my thoughts. I prayed that I was horribly mistaken but I knew it wasn't so.

He did not get in touch – not even to check whether I had got home safely. And I had to accept, at last, that he was not what he seemed. I was heartbroken and I could barely swallow my food – it felt as if a ball of anguish had lodged in my throat. I felt so vulnerable and out of my depth and longed to be my father's little girl once more.

He and I had some jolly times over the next few days, and we even went for a walk in Hyde Park together.

'You know, Sophia,' he said to me as we were strolling along arm-in-arm, 'I *am* very concerned about the cruel practices on the slave ships. If I – and many others – have our way, we will have this wretched trade banned! I feel that I have been too dismissive of your interest in the matter. Perhaps there is a place for the voices of intelligent young ladies, such as yourself, in political debate. You know, I would rather you came to me for advice than have you take it from strangers, darling.'

Dear Papa, he wasn't a monster at all. And to think how I had treated him!

As I sat reading a volume of the poems of William Wordsworth in the drawing room one morning in August, trying to distract my mind, Hawkes appeared to announce a guest.

'Who is it?' I asked.

'It is Lord Sandford, miss. Asking expressly for you,' said Hawkes, with one of his barely discernible winks.

'Oh dear!' I blurted out loud.

'Are you out, miss?' asked Hawkes.

'No, Hawkes. Please show him in,' I said. It was time I faced up to this other area of confusion in my life once and for all. It was some time since Estella's wedding, after all.

Lord Sandford was ushered in and I requested tea and fruit bread, before dismissing Hawkes.

'Miss Musgrove! How are you?' Lord Sandford asked.

'I am very well, thank you, Lord Sandford. It is good to see you,' I said politely.

'Perhaps we could walk in the garden together?' he suggested.

'Of course, if you wish,' I agreed, trying not to sound as nervous as I felt. I asked Annie to bring me a shawl, and told her that we would take our tea on the garden patio.

As we made our way through the scented bowers in the garden, Lord Sandford spoke very plainly.

'Miss Musgrove, I fear I have embarrassed myself, foolish man that I am,' he began. 'You see, I believed you were warmly disposed towards me, and that you would consider my proposal of marriage, made in a cowardly fashion through your father—' he went on.

'Lord Sandford,' I interrupted, 'this is all my fault. I fear I have misled you. I like you very much – as a friend. And as for Rose, she is a treasure. But I do not want to marry anyone just now.'

Lord Sandford smiled ruefully, embarrassed. 'I take the blame for this entirely . . .' he said.

I shook my head. 'No. It is my fault. I have a lot of thinking to do. You see, I fear I have behaved very badly of late,' I said, and I couldn't stop the tears from springing to my eyes.

'Oh, dear Miss Musgrove,' said Lord Sandford. 'Do not berate yourself. You have not treated me badly—'

'Thank you, but it is another matter that troubles me,' I said; it did indeed seem as if I had a host of problems heaped upon me.

'I see. Can I help you with it, Miss Musgrove? I have quite a bit of experience in life. My wife was a young lady of around your age when we met. She confused me at first with her many ups and downs, but I came to know her well. She was quite lovely. Very similar in looks to you. And in height and gracefulness too . . .' he told me.

'It is kind of you to offer to help me. You see, I have been ill used by a young man whose affections I sought. And I took something for him which was most wrong of me. Do you think I can possibly make things right again?' I asked.

Lord Sandford nodded. 'I am sure you can, with honesty and integrity – which you do not lack. One transgression is not the end of the world, my dear,' he said kindly.

I smiled through my tears.

'Am I to assume that we can remain friends despite our misunderstanding?' he asked me.

'Yes, of course!' I cried.

He kissed my hand just as my father arrived in the garden.

'Sophie! Sandford! Do I hear wedding bells?' Papa asked, sounding hopeful.

'No, Musgrove, we are good friends, that is all, regrettably,' Lord Sandford told him.

My poor father looked confused but let the matter rest, and I excused myself while they took tea together in the garden. No doubt they were saying what an unfathomable creature I am.

Lucy and Lady Lennox arrived soon after lunch.

'We saw Lord Sandford's carriage here earlier when we came to call,' exclaimed Lucy, 'and we turned away lest we should be interrupting anything!'

'No, no. We have sorted everything out and we are good friends,' I explained.

'That *is* good news!' said Lucy, taking my arm and pulling me towards the garden. 'Because, dear Sophie, I have some other news for you,' she said. 'Not such good news.'

'What news do you speak of, Lucy? Tell me please!' I implored.

'Well, I'm afraid I have learned much about your Mr Stevens of late. And it comes on good authority from my father's banker, Thomas Coutts on The

Strand,' Lucy whispered. 'By all accounts, Mr Stevens makes a habit of befriending wealthy young society beauties with sensitive natures, and extracting money or other favours from them. He uses good causes to persuade them to donate money, but he keeps the cash for himself, Sophie! This is how he finances his wealthy lifestyle. He is a con-man!'

My jaw dropped. 'But I was . . . You see, he said it was different . . . He was . . .' My voice trailed away as I finally realized that Marcus had indeed used me for his own ends, and that I had meant absolutely nothing to him all along.

'Mr Coutts says that Mr Stevens has used other ladies in this way – one being Mr Hughes's dear sister. But everyone avoids discussing his deeds for fear of scandal, you see,' said Lucy.

I shook my head in disbelief. I had ignored warnings from many people. From my father, from Mr Hughes, from Lucy – and from Lily too. I thought that I had known better than them all.

'Lucy, thank you for telling me the truth. It helps to dull the pain of rejection a little,' I said.

She hugged me. 'We both need some lessons in picking good men, don't we?' she said.

One morning soon after, Mrs Willow and I were

enjoying a stroll through the park on our way to the Maison du Chocolat.

'What will you wear to the Almack's autumn ball, Sophie dear? We must think of such things. There isn't much time left!' fretted Mrs Willow. 'Oh, I'll wear something I have already,' I said, unable to muster much enthusiasm for social events since the theatre party debacle. I was also distracted by a cloud of litter flying around us in the wind.

'It's shameful!' observed Mrs Willow. 'All these pieces of paper. I expect it's one of those nasty leaflet infestations!'

I was curious and stooped to pick up one of the fluttering sheets. But as soon as I read it, my blood ran cold. It was about the slave trade and used information from my father's confidential documents. They even made mention of 'Lord Musgrove' directly. I had been waiting for this moment and praying it would not come. Marcus had betrayed me in so many ways, it hurt like a knife turning in my heart. But had I not betrayed my father, this current treachery would not have been possible. It was all my fault. I choked back tears.

'What's wrong, Sophie?' asked Mrs Willow, seeing my distress.

'I'm afraid I need to turn back. I feel faint . . . I must rest, Mrs Willow,' I said.

She looked concerned but I did not stop to explain. Stuffing a few of the leaflets into my reticule, I turned on my heel and headed for home. At that moment it seemed as though my whole life was over.

Lucy was waiting for me at Musgrove House.

'Have you seen the leaflets?' I hissed as we tried to shake off Mrs Willow and Lady Lennox.

'No, do show me!' said Lucy.

'Remember our escapade in the Palace of Westminster? Well, the activists have used the information Mr Stevens sold to them for these,' I told her, handing over one of the papers I had picked up. 'The problem is that they quote Papa word for word, so he will be found guilty of indiscretion at the very least. See what I have done to my poor father!' I wailed.

Lucy read through the leaflet, shaking her head as she did so. 'You poor lamb. Mr Stevens was a villain and no mistake,' she said.

I sobbed into my handkerchief, unable to hold back my misery any longer.

'Ssshhh, Sophie. There, there. We all make mistakes, dear,' said Lucy. 'We'll get through it.'

'I'm sorry, but I keep thinking of more and more

harm that will come of this,' I sobbed. 'My mother will be devastated by my treachery!'

'But mothers understand all things, Sophie,' Lucy reassured me. 'You need to think of a plan of action. Come on, you're good at plans.'

At last my brain started to get to work on the problem. 'Well, I must confess it all to my father first and then make it up to him in whatever way I can,' I resolved.

'Good. Yes, that's an excellent start!' said Lucy encouragingly.

'Do you think it will damage his reputation terribly?' I asked.

'Maybe not. After all, *he* didn't sell the papers; they were stolen from him,' observed Lucy.

I winced as she reminded me of my deed with the word 'stolen'. The fact was that I had yet to face the music from Papa.

'At least we have the Almack's autumn ball soon!' said Lucy as cheerfully as possible as she left. But the ball was the last thing on my mind as I cuddled Dinky for comfort.

The next day I received a letter from my mother asking that I might join her at the Daisy Park for the last stages of her confinement. She said that Estella was coming and that I should bring Harry too. Papa was to follow as soon as he could.

Mrs Willow and I made plans to leave the next day, but I was determined to tell my father the truth about the stolen papers before our departure.

I packed for the reunion with my mother with the heaviest heart imaginable. I was worried about her giving birth and equally worried about the difficult conversation I must have with Papa.

Chapter Twenty-one

As I prepared to leave Musgrove House, my father came to talk to me in my room.

'Sophie, I have something to tell you, but you must not concern your mother with it,' he began. 'You and I have formed a more grown-up bond of late, and I know you do not want to be sheltered from my political life, so I wish to tell you this. Some of my private government documents have been stolen and used for political propaganda. I have been most terribly compromised. I am shouldering the blame, and my head is on the chopping block, so to speak,' he said. 'It might be the end of my political career. The Prime Minister is furious with me.'

I knew that this was my opportunity to tell the truth. 'Papa,' I said, 'that is too terrible. But I have something to tell you too . . .' I looked away and took a deep breath. 'It was me, Papa. I took the papers to help those opposing the slave trade. I am so sorry. It was the most dreadful thing to do and I am terribly ashamed of myself. I didn't know the material would be used in this way, but I should have guessed. Can you ever forgive me? I know it is a dreadful thing to have done and I regret it more than I can say.'

My father looked aghast. He turned every shade of grey. 'My own Sophie? *You* did this? But how did you get the papers?' he asked.

'I stole your spare keys and went to your room at the Palace of Westminster,' I confessed.

My father held his head in his hands for what seemed like a very long time.

'It was as if I was different person, Papa. I am so filled with regret . . . Please forgive me,' I begged, breaking down in sobs. 'I cannot bear the idea that you will not forgive me.'

'Let your mother know nothing of this. Ever!' my father said, his voice full of emotion. 'She is delicate. If I were to lose her . . .' He seemed to choke on his words.

'Papa, I will not breathe a word of it – and for her sake, not mine,' I agreed.

'Now, I wish to be alone,' he said quietly as he rose to leave my room. 'I need time to think.'

I nodded and sank down on my bed, distraught. My father, the man I had so misunderstood, was actually filled with honour, taking the blame for the leaks, and concerned only for his wife's health. I was wretched with self-disgust.

He didn't speak to me again until I was in the carriage, ready to depart for the Cotswolds with Mrs Willow and Harry. Then he came running out to speak to me. 'Sophie. Before you go,' he said, 'I forgive you. We all make mistakes. But I need to know that you will never, ever do anything like this again. I could not overlook it a second time. Come – promise me, Sophie. We must not break your mother's heart with a feud between us,' he added.

I hugged him with all my might. 'Thank you, Papa – and I promise that I will never, ever let you down again,' I sobbed.

'What *are* you two going on about?' asked Harry.

Mrs Willow smiled. 'Well, isn't that nice?' she said, looking pleased that the differences between father and daughter seemed to have been resolved. And then she tactfully turned away to distract Harry with a game of I Spy.

When we arrived at the Daisy Park, the household was in a great flap. My mother was already in labour!

Estella was at Mama's bedside and Mrs Willow went in to assist. I was not allowed into the bedroom, so I tried to busy myself with some gardening chores while Harry darted about, trying to make a boat float on the lake and collecting insects in a glass jar.

When Harry and I returned to the house a few hours later, my mother was still in labour and I was overcome with worry. I tried listening at the door but the sounds I heard made me retreat hastily. My mother was a frail lady in her early forties. Could she possibly survive this terrible ordeal?

'Is Mama going to die?' asked Harry as we toyed with our scrambled eggs at tea time.

'No, Harry. She has the best medical care,' I told him, trying to sound reassuring. 'But it is a very slow affair, producing a baby. I'm sure it was the same when you were born, and when Estella and I were too. Try to think of other things, darling,' I said.

He did not look convinced. The poor boy had reached an age when he realized that not everything he was told was strictly true.

Eventually, as darkness fell, Mrs Willow came out into the hallway and called for me. 'Sophie! Come and meet your new baby sister!' she cried. 'And Harry too!'

We tiptoed eagerly into the room to see my

mother cradling a tiny, perfect baby in her arms.

'Mama! You are well!' I exclaimed, and kissed the sleeping baby. 'She's quite beautiful! I love her!'

Harry looked on with a bemused expression. 'She's very nice indeed,' he said, 'but I won't come close until after my bath.'

'What shall we call her?' I asked.

'Your father and I like Constance. Connie for short,' Mama replied.

I stared and stared at Connie. I had never seen such an exquisite creature in all my life. She was plump and pink, with fair hair and violet-blue eyes. Her fingers and toes and ears looked so tiny.

'She's just like me!' declared Estella, who looked very worn out. She had seen enough of the birth to declare that she would be childless for life.

'No, she's not like you. She's just like me!' objected Harry.

'How can she be like you, Harry, when she's so sweet?' I teased. And Mama laughed merrily and her face grew young once more.

'Did we all make you feel so ill when we were being hatched, Mama?' I asked.

'Yes, only I was younger and stronger then. But every time has been worth it, when I consider the end results,' she replied.

We all felt as though it was our job to present our baby as favourably as possible to Papa, when he arrived the next day. We were all washed and smartly dressed as we sat with Mama and Constance, awaiting his arrival.

'I hope she doesn't cry when Papa first sees her. He thinks he makes all babies burst into tears!' said Harry as he stroked our darling little sister's tiny hand.

While we were waiting, little Rose Sandford came to visit with her nurse, Ginny. She was amazed and delighted with Connie, longing to hold her and push her in her carriage.

'Papa has a new friend!' Rose announced as I showed her the pretty new nursery set up at the Daisy Park. 'She is called Miss Adams, and she's very pretty! I think he *loves* her!'

I breathed a sigh of relief. 'How wonderful, Rose. It is nice to have special friends,' I told her.

'Can I whisper a secret to you?' asked Rose.

'Of course,' I replied and bent down to receive the message.

'Papa kissed Miss Adams once. They didn't know I was looking!' Rose told me.

I smiled. 'Best to keep that a secret, Rose, don't you think?' I said. And she nodded in a way that made me think others had already been told the secret too.

I was pleased to hear that Lord Sandford was happy. He was such a good man. At last it seemed as though some of the black clouds over me were lifting.

There was nothing that had ever depressed me quite so much as being a deceiver. As for Marcus, I had heard nothing from him since the ill-fated party at the King's Theatre. I supposed I was of no use to him now. In some moods, I wished he would write and be full of good wishes to me, but on the whole I thought that I was better off without him. Those who had said I was being led astray had been quite right. But the confusing thing was that I still desperately wanted to help stop the slave trade.

Rose and Ginny headed home and at last my father arrived at the Daisy Park. We ushered him into Mama's bedroom. He walked over to the bed and embraced her, and I am sure I saw tears of joy on his cheek as he looked at his new daughter.

He was simply enchanted by Connie. I was a little jealous for a moment when I saw him fall in love with her, I confess! He held her in his arms and she cooed and gurgled happily.

Papa was very mindful of the fact that little Harry had lost his role of baby-in-residence. He took him riding the next day and they built a camp in the woods beside the house. We spent a couple of blissful weeks at the Daisy Park, enjoying getting to know the baby, and being a united family once more.

But by early September it seemed that the whole Musgrove family was ready to move back to the city again for the autumn Season. Estella wanted to come with us too.

'What do we do?' I heard Papa say to Mama. 'She is our child and she is not happy with her husband at Dovetail Hall. I say let her come to London and we will see if he chases her. Perhaps he can change his ways and correct his behaviour!'

So, to my delight, Estella came to London with us too.

Chapter Twenty-two

We arrived back at Musgrove House in the early autumn. The plums were ripe on the trees and the air had a little nip in the mornings and evenings. It was really too wonderful for words to be in the main family home with both my parents and my three siblings. I was still worried about my father's career, but at least I had no secrets from him now. My complete happiness was blighted only by these worries for Papa and my thoughts of Lily and how she was prospering.

I asked Hawkes for her address one morning, and as he wrote it down, we were disturbed by the sound of the doorbell.

I ran into the receiving room, tidying my hair and pinching my cheeks for colour. Hawkes announced the arrival of a visitor. Lucy had been to see Connie lately, so I knew it could not be her. In fact, Lucy and

Lady Lennox had visited three times of late, so delighted were they with the new addition to our family.

'It's Mr Hughes,' said Hawkes.

He swept into our receiving room, looking quite sun-kissed from a trip to Greece on some sort of military business.

We settled down to chat, quite alone apart from the occasional appearance of Harry, who was careering around the house on a two-wheeled scooter contraption which the coachmen had helped him make. One of the plus points of the new baby was that Mrs Willow was quite obsessed with her, and did not like the young nurses to have sole charge of her – so she quite forgot about me at times.

'I hear that you have a new addition to the family,' said Mr Hughes. 'I have brought a gift from my family for her.'

'Oh, that is kind,' I said, accepting a pretty pink parcel from him. 'Would you like to see her?'

'Very much. Although I fear she will hate the look of me – they all do!' he said, sounding just like my father!

When we presented Connie to him, she cooed and lay happily in his arms. 'I think I shall take her home!' he announced, to which Harry replied: 'Indeed you shall not!'

Ever since Mr Hughes had rescued me on the night of the party, I had felt warmly towards him. I suppose I should have felt rather embarrassed at seeing him again, but there was no sense of drama about him, just a steady and thoughtful presence that left me feeling quite serene and able to chat in an easy way.

When Mr Hughes finally left, I had an odd feeling – as though I would miss him and eagerly anticipate the next time we met.

Over the next two weeks I had time to think about my recent experiences and I realized I had some unfinished business to attend to in order to put my world straight again. Firstly I asked my father if we could invite Lily back into our employment.

'Of course, I don't know if she'll want to come back,' I told him.

'Well, you must be humble – you must go to her home and meet her face to face. And another thing, Sophie,' he cautioned. 'We don't want to hurt Annie's feelings, now do we?'

'No, Papa. Of course not. What shall I say to her?' I asked.

'Well, let's see what Lily says and then we can break the news very gently to Annie if necessary,' he suggested.

I nodded, took on board all that he said, and a few days later went to visit Lily in person.

Mrs Willow and I set off for the Whitechapel area, with Sid driving us. Luckily he knew exactly where to go.

I had known that it would be a difficult experience, but I was not prepared for what I saw. As we left the smart West End behind, my eyes grew large at the sights before me. It was as if we were entering another land. I wrinkled up my nose at the smells of rotten fish and vegetables, as well as the raw sewage that ran along the sides of the cobbled streets. Mrs Willow held her handkerchief over her nose.

Children with ragged clothes and bare feet were begging for food, and the tiny one- or two-roomed houses were tightly packed together as if fighting for space. As we slowed down, it dawned on me that Lily must live in one such house.

The children must have been drawn to the Musgrove carriage as a symbol of wealth, for they cried out for food and pennies as soon as we stopped. I threw out all I had, and wished I had brought more to give.

'Lily!' I cried when I saw my former maid washing clothes in a barrel by the door of her little house. I recalled that she had once told me that twenty people lived in her house, though I could hardly believe it when I saw how tiny it was.

She looked up in surprise, followed by joy, which was quickly replaced by extreme embarrassment. 'Miss Sophia! What are you doing here? It's not safe for you!' she gasped.

Dear Lily – always thinking of my safety! She's such a gem. I got out of the carriage.

'Hello, Lily. I am here to talk to you. May I come inside?' I asked, seeing that we were surrounded by onlookers – mainly children and elderly people; working-age people would be in the factories, I assumed. Or maybe in the ale houses.

'Er, yes, miss, but it's very cramped and damp,' Lily said nervously. 'But please come inside, of course.'

Leaving Mrs Willow to wait in the carriage, I followed Lily into the main room, which was terribly dingy and stuffed with objects – though I could see her light touch in the neat piles of things and the thin curtains at the tiny window.

Lily cleared a wooden chair for me to sit on, which I accepted. 'May I fetch you a cup of ale, miss?' she asked.

'No, thank you, Lily,' I replied, clearing my throat. 'I am here to say sorry and to ask you if you would come back to Musgrove House. We miss you, and I realize I was wrong to be so cross with you. I have been very foolish of late, but I have learned a lesson, and I am so very sorry,' I explained tearfully.

I thought I would have a hard job on my hands, but Lily fell to her knees beside me and said: 'Oh, thank you, Miss Sophie. We are all finding it hard here as I used to send most of my wages home. And now my brother Arthur might lose his job at the candle factory, and, well . . . of course I'll come back! I've missed you too! Anyway, I know I was wrong to tell your father your secrets. And I'm sorry for it too.'

'Oh, Lily. You were just concerned, and you were right to be worried! I will tell you how it all turned out in due course. But thank you for agreeing to come back. It is excellent news!'

'I've been thinking about a new hair-do for you as well,' Lily said eagerly. 'I saw it in a magazine what my neighbour got from her mistress over in the West End!'

I laughed. 'I can't wait for you to try it out on me, Lily!' I said. 'I am thrilled that you will come back to us. And of course, we have a new baby now!' I told her.

'Ooh, yes – how lovely, miss. When can I come back? And what is the baby called? And what's been happening? And how's Miss Lucy?' she said all at once.

We laughed and fell into each other's arms. 'Come back and I will tell you *everything*!' I said.

Lily packed a little bag and jumped into the carriage after saying farewell to her family.

As we travelled back towards Mayfair, I realized that although I was still concerned about the slave trade (and will be, until it is no more), I was also worried about the starving on the streets of London too. I was beginning to see that there were many kinds of suffering out there. My broken heart seemed a trifling problem compared to some. I was more determined than ever to help change the world for the better, but I resolved to treat those I loved with more respect while I was doing so.

Lily danced back into Musgrove House and made a beeline for the baby. I do believe that Mrs Willow was rather jealous when she proved to be popular with little Connie!

Once Lily was back in her rightful place as my personal hairdresser, we discussed my remaining worry. My father was still shouldering the blame for the leaked documents and was due to meet the Prime

Minister to receive his punishment now that he was back from the Daisy Park. I asked Lily if she thought I should go and confess what I had done to the Prime Minister himself.

She knew about most of my idiotic behaviour, but she had not realized quite how low I had stooped with the theft of the papers.

'Lily, do you think it will be all right to go behind my father's back one last time?' I asked her. 'I want to be totally honest about what I've done and not try and sweep it away,' I explained.

She thought it over for a while. 'I agree that in future total honesty is the best policy, miss,' she said at last, 'but perhaps one last deception is just about all right.'

One day shortly after this, just before I made my visit to help clear my father's name, Mrs Willow and I went on a shopping spree to purchase some new items for baby Connie. At last we could indulge ourselves in Bennets, the delightful baby outfitters in Mayfair. We chose a wonderful layette of white brushed-cotton baby gowns, knitted jackets, hats and tiny socks. It was lovely to know that Mama and the baby were both well. I had never seen Mrs Willow so happy.

Of course, her other pet subject was Almack's ball, and our conversation soon turned to that.

'Wouldn't it be wonderful if you got engaged soon? After Almack's would be perfect!' Mrs Willow trilled as we got into the carriage.

'But to whom, exactly? You just want rid of me to have more time with Connie, don't you?' I teased.

'Well, she is less testy, I must admit. But no – I just fear that Mr Hughes won't wait for you for ever,' she replied. 'A man has his pride.'

I tutted. Mr Hughes and I? Engaged! What an improbable thought.

On our way back to the carriage, we passed a news-stand with the day's newspapers displayed. As usual there was a billboard with the day's main story. I stopped in my tracks as I read the headline: ANTI-SLAVERY CAMPAIGNERS IMPRISONED FOR VIOLENT ATTACK!

'Mrs Willow, may we buy a newspaper please?' I asked.

We stopped and paid for *The Times*.

As we settled into the carriage, I scanned the front page. I could not believe it. Diana and two others from the anti-slavery group had attacked Viscount Castlereagh as he left the Palace of Westminster. It said:

In an entirely unprovoked attack, the militant trio pulled the peer to the ground and battered his face and body with heavy sticks. He was left for dead and can only recall the group chanting the words: *Die of shame!*

An onlooker managed to alert the guards, who ran to the Viscount's rescue. They gave chase and brought down the attackers, arresting them and throwing them into Westminster gaol . . .

I gasped.

'Are you all right, Sophie?' asked Mrs Willow.

I nodded. 'I'll be fine.' I had certainly flirted with danger to please Marcus. I wondered what he was doing now . . . Obviously he had not been part of the passionate protest which had landed Diana in gaol. Had he *ever* cared about the plight of slaves? I wondered.

Chapter Twenty-three

I had never had any doubts about my plan to visit the Prime Minister but the news story stiffened my resolve further. I had learned that cruel acts cannot be countered with further cruelty. I dressed myself smartly for my visit and consoled myself that this was the last time I would do anything behind my father's back.

I had met the Prime Minister several times at Musgrove House, and liked him well. When I arrived at White Lodge in Richmond Park, I was shown into his personal office.

It was a dark room with rich, forest-green walls and Chesterfield sofas. A general sense of solemnity hung over it. The Prime Minster's desk was vast, with several inkwells upon it and neatly filed papers in coloured boxes. It smacked of a busy man, but an orderly one.

The Prime Minster rose to greet me and took my hand. 'This is an unusual meeting, Miss Musgrove,' he said. 'Please sit down.'

I sat on a sofa and he joined me there. I looked at his powdered grey wig and strong features. His nose was almost Roman, but there was no cruelty in his face. His eyes were large and kind, if a little weary, framed by heavy brows.

'I know this is out of the ordinary, and I must thank you for seeing me. I am here to make a confession,' I told him, coming straight to the point.

He looked confused, so I told him about my role in the leaking of the papers. I defended Papa's integrity and assured Mr Addington of his allegiance to him. I also told him of my burning desire to help put an end to the slave trade.

The Prime Minister looked quite stern. 'Stealing those confidential papers was a most terrible thing to do, Miss Musgrove, wasn't it?'

I agreed wholeheartedly.

'You have behaved like a common criminal. And the crime is against your own papa. Shocking!' he said gravely.

I hung my head.

'But it is brave of you to come here,' he went on.

'Wise too.' He rose and paced the room. 'You are trying to clear your father's name. For that I commend you. I knew he would not have sold secrets for money as some believed, but I could not fathom the spring of the leak at all.' He sat at his desk and took out a sheet of paper, making notes as he spoke.

'So, you have explained much that was troubling me,' he continued. 'As for your concern for the slaves, it is commendable. These issues keep me awake at night too. We have tried to end the trade, but to do so we must tackle all the roots and thorns of it, bit by stubborn bit.'

I nodded. 'I have no doubt that it is a trickier situation than I first realized,' I assured him. 'At first I thought that the radical approach was the only answer, but now I know it is entirely wrong. Two wrongs will never make a right, will they, sir?'

'Indeed not!' he replied firmly.

'Perhaps debates and bills and small steps forward are the only ways,' I said.

'You know, Miss Musgrove, there are a few fine ladies like yourself who campaign peacefully and gracefully for such causes – such as Elizabeth Heyrick and Anne Knight. I suggest you become involved with them, and avoid the more . . . shall we say, *rascally* elements of the campaigning fraternity,' Mr Addington said.

'That sounds like an excellent idea, sir,' I replied. 'And as for my father, he loves his political work and has done no wrong – except to bring up a wayward daughter,' I added.

The Prime Minister smiled. 'Let's say a highly spirited one, shall we?'

I rose to leave. 'Thank you for your time. And my sincere apologies for my extremely bad behaviour. I can only beg for forgiveness again.'

'Miss Musgrove, you are indeed a strong-minded girl. I would like to ask you how you got into the Palace of Westminster to execute your mission, but I am worried that I would find the details all too enthralling.'

'It is a sorry story,' I admitted. 'Rest assured that it shall not happen again.' We shook hands. I could only hope that all this meant that my father's neck was off the chopping block.

It was now late September, and we had been back in London for three weeks. I was finally getting excited about the autumn ball at Almack's and there were all sorts of things to be done. I had to have fittings – as I had agreed to a new gown after all – Lily insisted on trying out a new hairstyle on me, and I had to choose my jewellery.

Besides all this, Estella helped me with other preparations such as deportment exercises, herbal preparations and walks in the fresh air to improve the complexion. She and I loved having each other for company again. Harry had now returned to The Glebe.

'You are happier without Mr Dovetail, aren't you, dearest?' I said to Estella on one of our walks.

'It is true, but I will see if it can work out in time. I cannot give up so soon!' she replied with a sigh.

'Well, if he comes to live with us, we can check him when he is cruel. And we will!' I assured her.

She nodded. In fact, we had a surprise at supper that evening, for Mr Dovetail appeared before us with no prior warning of his arrival. I thought poor Estella would die of fright.

Papa drew himself up and asked him what he meant by shocking us in this fashion.

'I am sorry, sir,' he replied. 'I was concerned that I might be refused the opportunity to see my wife if I announced my plans in advance.'

Papa simply shook his head and replied, 'Be seated and join us for dinner.'

I tried to make polite conversation throughout the

meal for Estella's sake, but it was not easy: I felt that Mr Dovetail had helped to lure me into the clutches of Mr Stevens with his tall tales of how wonderful the man was. Surely he must have known he was a blackguard? But then again, Mr Dovetail is not blessed with the sharpest of brains, so perhaps he had no inkling. I couldn't be sure, but I felt that perhaps he had learned a lesson since Estella had rejoined the Musgrove fold. He certainly seemed to be making an effort that evening, but was he the type to unlearn a lesson just as fast as he'd picked it up?

Whatever my misgivings, it was decided between Papa and Estella that Mr Dovetail would stay on as our guest for a while. I was relieved that we would be able to keep an eye on him and happy that I could still enjoy my sister's company.

The next day, as if there wasn't enough going on, we were all of a twitter – for the Queen came to see Connie! It is true that Queen Charlotte adores babies, but I was worried that she was going to make noises about my mother returning to Court as well. Mama is unusual in that she has nursed all her babies herself, so I hoped that as long as Connie was reliant on her for nourishment, we would be safe.

Queen Charlotte and Princess Amelia spent a

whole jolly afternoon with us, admiring the baby and playing with her. As the Queen rose to leave, I held my breath, waiting for a comment about Court life.

'Farewell, Maria,' she said. 'Let me know when Connie is weaned and we can see you once more at Kew.'

Mama merely smiled and bid the royal pair farewell.

Meanwhile my father was invited to meet the Prime Minister. It was several days since my own meeting with Mr Addington, and I waited anxiously for Papa to return, pacing around so much that I got on Mrs Willow's nerves.

'Sit down and read! What vexes you?' she asked as she cuddled Connie in her arms.

'Nothing, Mrs Willow. I am thinking, that is all,' I replied.

'Well, why not just *be* for a change? You are thinking too much for my liking!' she retorted. I was even getting on Dinky's nerves. He loves to follow me, but I was pacing so much he couldn't keep up and went to lie in his basket.

At last Papa came home and immediately asked to see me in private. We went into the library.

'Is everything all right, Papa?' I asked him as he sat in his favourite winged armchair.

He motioned for me to sit down opposite him. 'Yes, Sophie. I am to lie low for a further month and then resume my normal duties. In actual fact, I am finding this break from work quite refreshing with little Connie around,' he added. 'Oh, and Sophia, the Prime Minister thinks you have quite a career ahead of you in politics!'

'Papa, that visit was my last secret from you, I promise!' I said.

'I doubt it will be, but you must never betray me or those who love you *ever* again. Do you understand that, dear daughter?' he asked.

I nodded. 'Papa, you have my word,' I assured him.

'And I promise I will be more of a champion of the under-privileged in future,' he told me. 'And I will involve you more in my work.'

'So I haven't been completely wicked these past few months?' I asked nervously.

He looked thoughtful. 'No, you have done a great deal to shake things about. But wicked, no,' he said, shaking his head. 'Now, I have a baby to cuddle!' he added, and charged up to the nursery.

I was still sitting there, thinking through our

conversation, when he suddenly burst back into the library and hugged me awkwardly. 'Mustn't forget about the older babies too,' he muttered.

The night of Almack's autumn ball arrived at last and I could not have been more excited – especially now that the chaos I had created in my life had largely been put to rights, and my darling mother was fit and well.

Lucy and I wanted to arrive at the ball together, so Mrs Willow, Estella, Mr Dovetail and I went in our coach to collect Lucy and Lady Lennox. Mrs Willow and Lady Lennox looked quite splendid. Mrs Willow wore a lavender satin gown with lace trim, while the normally rather drab Lady Lennox looked delicate in softest rose-pink.

Of course Lucy looked wonderful in a white cape worn over a clear sky-blue unstructured gown, and my sister was a picture in Wedgwood green satin.

I wore my beautiful new gown – which was of French design in a soft shade of duck-egg blue, the fabric falling in chiffon folds from a high waist. Lily had surpassed herself with the most exquisite of hair-styles for me. Dear Estella said it would set a new trend it was so lovely. Instead of ringlets, my dark hair was swept up into an elegant chignon, and then a few soft tendrils were allowed to fall onto my face.

I didn't know what to expect from the evening or who would be there, although it was safe to assume that everyone in high society, returning from their summer breaks in the country, would attend.

'Oh, Sophie, isn't this nice? Back to our old ways,' said Lucy as we all climbed into the large coach, with three rows of seats.

'Here, here,' muttered Mrs Willow.

We all laughed merrily together as Lucy led us in a sing-song based around a rhyme she had made up about all the odd people at the top of London society. She insisted we all sing the chorus, which went:

> *The Royals are bad:*
> *Our King is mad,*
> *His son's a cad,*
> *His wife is sad . . .*

Even Mr Dovetail seemed to be on good form that night, and his mean streak was much less evident anyway since he'd been staying with us in London. Before we knew it, we had arrived at Almack's, which was bright with lanterns and torches at the entrance.

There were sounds of giggles and chattering all around as we made our way up the vast staircase towards the ballroom. The whole place was decorated with autumn flowers and golden decorations. We gave our capes to a door girl and were issued with a number for them.

The band was playing cheerful dance music. We paraded along beside the dance floor, as one must, and found that our dance cards began to fill up quite quickly.

I hardly dared confess to myself that I was feeling rather disappointed Mr Hughes was not there. I looked around for him, over heads and in vast mirrors, but he was nowhere to be seen. Then, midway through a cotillion with a pleasant but un-inspiring gentleman called Mr Palmer, I caught sight of him at the edge of the dance floor. My cheeks felt as though they were on fire, so I quickly looked away. I couldn't be sure he would come to talk to me after the dance, but I was determined to regain some composure in case he did.

I curtsied at the end of the dance and went back to join Mrs Willow, Estella and Mr Dovetail.

'He's coming over!' whispered Estella.

'Who is?' I asked nonchalantly.

'Why, Mr Hughes, of course!' she replied.

'Oh, him,' I said, admiring my pretty bracelet as he approached. I was desperate to conceal the flush in my cheeks that betrayed how pleased I was to see him.

'Good evening,' he said to us all. 'I trust you are well, Miss Musgrove?' he added, turning to me.

'Oh, yes. Very well indeed, thank you,' I replied.

'Do you have any spaces on your dance card?' he asked.

'Er, yes, three spaces, Mr Hughes, it would seem,' I told him.

'How fortunate. I was planning to dance exactly three times this evening, Miss Musgrove, so it seems we are fated to dance together thrice,' he concluded.

I smiled. 'Well, I look forward to seeing you after the next dance in that case,' I replied. He bowed and left us at that point.

'Well done, Sophie,' said Mrs Willow. 'That is better behaviour!'

I rolled my eyes. 'He has no romantic interest in me, and I have none in him,' I told her emphatically. 'We are just friends.'

I suppose I am quite a good dancer, even though I never go to the classes I'm supposed to attend. I certainly enjoyed dancing with Mr Hughes, who is also a fine dancer when he can be bothered to try.

Thankfully, he was too discreet to mention the King's Theatre incident, and though I worried that I might seem dull, we chatted together so easily that the three cotillions passed in the blink of an eye.

He took me back to my seat and bade us all goodnight.

'You are leaving already, Mr Hughes?' said Estella. 'Is the ball not to your taste?'

'I came to dance three times, and now that is done, there is no more pleasure to be had,' he explained with a small smile and a bow.

We all watched him leave, and apart from Lucy, who was dancing with the sons of *all* the English nobles, we felt rather deflated when he was gone.

'I have bored him! See, Mrs Willow! When I behave nicely, I am dull!' I said, teasing her.

'He said that all his pleasure was over after the three dances. I take that to mean he enjoyed the dances, Sophia,' she observed.

'He thinks me a silly child,' I protested, remembering the night of the rescue from the theatre. And, indeed, I did wonder how he could take me seriously after that embarrassing escapade.

I went out for some air and saw Leonora Pink in conversation with Mr Hughes near the carriages. They looked like a lovely couple and I did not want them to think I was spying so I went back inside.

As the evening wore on, I was confirmed in my long-held belief that balls are not for me. I wanted to have deep conversations with fascinating people, discover some great eternal truth – or at least whirl around the dance floor properly with a gentleman like Mr Hughes who really knows how to dance! But the endless jigs with the vapid young men that one mostly has to endure at a ball? No, thank you.

In the carriage on the way home, I bored everyone with my analysis of Mr Hughes's behaviour. 'If he liked me, he would have stayed to watch me,' I observed.

'Or perhaps seeing you dance with other men drives him wild with jealousy!' Lucy suggested.

I shook my head. 'He isn't the jealous type.'

'Until now!' she shot back.

'No, I think he simply wanted to be polite,' I decided.

'Time will tell,' offered Mrs Willow, boringly.

'But I want to know right now!' I wailed. Then I recovered my decorum. 'I mean, I don't care one way or another about him, but a girl has to know where she stands,' I concluded.

Everyone smiled and looked out of the window –

even Mr Dovetail, who did not dare to comment on such delicate matters.

Thankfully, dear Lucy soon distracted everyone with a risqué joke she had heard at the ball.

I spent the next few days wondering what Mr Hughes might be doing, and what he really thought of me, and I found myself absently sketching him when I took my drawing pad out into the garden. 'Stop this nonsense, Sophie!' I told myself. 'He thinks you are no more than a silly little girl!'

A week later Lucy and I met at Harvey's coffee house to discuss our forthcoming appointments while Mrs Willow and Lady Lennox chatted happily together.

We had brought all our latest invitations so that we could open them together.

'What do we have for next weekend?' I asked.

'Well, I have a Saturday salon in Greenwich with the poet Samuel Coleridge,' Lucy said.

'Let me open this one,' I said. 'Oh, we have a clash!' I exclaimed. 'We are asked to a weekend house party at Mr Hughes's country home. Whatever shall we do?' I wondered, secretly more interested in the prospect of seeing Mr Hughes again, and enjoying his easy conversation, than in a poetry salon.

'Oooh, Greenwich, definitely!' teased Lucy. 'I love the works of Coleridge.'

'Very well,' I agreed nobly.

'Although, it *might* be fun to see Mr Hughes's country house. I've heard it is quite splendid,' Lucy went on.

'Very well, Mr Hughes's it is then,' I concluded. 'Just to be polite – since he saved my life!' I added.

'Of course, just to be polite!' giggled Lucy. 'Why, Sophie Musgrove! I do believe you are blushing!'

'Nonsense. He really isn't my type,' I said firmly.

Lucy clearly decided to let it go. 'Are you done with campaigning?' she asked, sweetly changing the subject.

'Not exactly. I have some important work to do for Lily's brother. He has been bullied by a horrid factory owner, you see, and I thought we could—'

'Oh, no! No more secret missions!' said Lucy, throwing her gloves at me playfully.

I caught them and laughed. 'Don't worry, I am going to approach life more carefully from now on,' I assured her. 'And there's going to be a lot more dancing and a lot less deception.'

'I should think so!' she said with a smile.

And so we sipped our hot chocolates and chatted merrily about our other invitations, and which outfits to take to Mr Hughes's weekend house party, and my life felt more full of hope and happiness than it had in some time.

'Lucy, about the house party . . .' I began, once all our fashion decisions had been made.

Lucy nodded enquiringly.

'I'm only going if Dinky can come too!' I said.